Letters from a Shuttered Country

Chris Steed

Contents

Chapter One:

In Which the Story Ends

An unremarkable bungalow in an unremarkable street.

A key turned in the lock.

"Hey, Dad!"

Nothing. She called again. The heavens were as brass.

The kitchen was smart, the lounge surprisingly shabby, the dining room functional. This was home for a while as Katie Trimble hunkered down to isolate with her dad while the sale of her own flat had to be put on ice. She wandered around wondering where he was. Then she heard sounds from upstairs.

"I'm up here," came a voice she knew and loved.

"You had me worried there for a minute," Kate exclaimed. "Shall I come up?"

"I'll be down," Bill called out. But his voice sounded like a muffled drum. "Give me a minute. And by the way, put the kettle on if you would. There's a love."

And when Bill came down, he wore the look of someone who hadn't been weeping but you think there was enough feeling to warrant a box of tissues.

"Dad!" Kate caught his face. "Whatever is the matter?"

"I'll be all right love," came the reply. But his voice was heavy with emotion.

"Now where's that tea?"

"Thanks for bringing the shopping in." Bill was really grateful. In Covid UK, the queue stretched to infinity and beyond. Well, not exactly, but he had spent seventy minutes trying to get to the supermarket the other day. Standing two metres apart, his fellow shoppers were compatriots in crisis before returning to their troglodyte world.

"How was school?" Bill asked.

"Not a single child we are concerned about attended school today," said Katie pensively. "I'm highly concerned about one particular child. Charlie has a couple of brothers and sisters. The Mum screams in their face for no reason. Her boyfriend screams at her all day long."

"Bad business", said Bill, shaking his head. "If your family is struggling in the first place, things are going to snap with this virus."

"How do we make sure the children that should be at school are safe?" asked Katie quizzically. "They'll be spending more time online and that's a Wild West sometimes. But look, what's up?"

"Think you mean 'What's App'?" Bill smiled.

Two cups of tea teased. "Come on," said Katie. "How about if we do our daily exercise?" "Aren't you the lucky one living so close to the sea!"

What an extraordinary moment this was in our national life! The old times, when you could do what you wanted without thinking twice, seemed to be a receding memory. Destabilising, confusing – we didn't know how to be or what to do. Normal sources of solace were severely restricted. But you could go for daily exercise. More than ever, they felt very laden with gifts that the Channel was within walking distance.

By now, the sun had more than halved the day. Small flaky mists crept along the edges of the surrounding hills. There was hardly anyone about. Were they lone survivors and a flood had silently engulfed the old order of things? Everything lay bathed in eerie silence. Shutters had come down, it seemed, on everything you could access from home.

Life was lived invisibly. Yet, behind shuttered doors lay a tardis of activity. The world outside was denied except for the brief foray into reality. Inside, at the click of a mouse, adventures were to be had; adventures without touch. But what was real – the shuttered life of physicality or the galaxy of the mouse? There was much to hold on to.

Twenty years had now passed. Bill was struggling to recollect things these days. Even the face of Ali seemed to slip away elusively in the corridors of memory.

"Found a whole load of letters today amidst dozens of documents," said Bill at last.

"And?" asked Katie. "You've got to tell me now, Dad," she said, aware of his reticence.

To his daughter's loving concern, Bill succumbed. He gave her a one-minute headline.

"Write to them again," Katie urged. "Now we are in Covid lock-down, get back in touch. It's not as if you are busy with other things. I'm sure you've got their e-mails somewhere or could look them up on Zoom." She touched him affectionately on the shoulder.

"I might just do that," Bill replied heavily. "I'd like to make contact again."

Ten minutes later, they stood on a hillside on the south coast of England. Where the river carved its way into the sea, a town had once sprung up. Fishing had been the main means of support for many hundreds of years. Here, tourists came in their thousands, attracted by the calm beauty of the bay and the water that sometimes lapped gently against the seashore, sometimes driven with ferocity and power.

Had they been allowed, the route to the sea lay nearly a mile along the footpath. Their footfall made a quiet echo on the hillside. Up a little, further along, past rows of hedges and the top of the sea, Bill and Katie paused to draw breath and take in the scenes that begged to be described. Painters and photographers had been drawn here, to capture the soft landscape and offer it to others. Splashes of brown and reds broke up the many greens that paraded on a Spring morning. How many types of green could there be?

But that was enough of the outdoors today. It was time to go back indoors, to retreat into the interior life. Katie managed to open her father up a little.

"You can read them if you want," volunteered Bill. "Wonder how you see it all? What with all this time on our hands, thought I would have a bit of a clear-out. To be honest with you, I'd forgotten these old letters were there."

But many other things had been sparked off and were jumping back into memory. He thought of another Easter or two. After Katie had settled down that eve, she wondered what this pile of papers would yield? Would she learn very much and make the jigsaw pattern of his mysterious past come at last to a picture that made sense?

Passover, 1999. Israel. The land of the sherut, the shared taxi. At Ben Gurion airport, the four friends passed through immigration, collected their luggage and then piled into a taxi with two other men. At ten dollars per person, this was good value.

One of their companions, a bearded American, leaned forward in greeting.

"Hi, the name's Dave."

"Are you a pilgrim?" Steve asked him laconically.

"I'm an End Timer," replied the first fellow traveller.

"A what?" asked Steve.

"AIDS; natural disasters! There's a whirlwind of judgement visiting the Earth at this hour of history. Jerusalem is where the action is about to happen. It's time now for God to intervene."

The second fellow-traveller shook his head in disgust. "It's the Jerusalem syndrome," he said. "It's bringing out all the crazies. Do you know what I've just been asked at immigration? 'Have you come to commit suicide?' If you are single, from a Christian country and not in a regular tour programme, they think you're a loony! Had to show them my return flight."

After the 50-kilometre drive and an incessant blaring of horns, they found themselves once more in the most fascinating city in the world. If it did not live up to its Hebrew name, 'City of Peace', the Arabic name for Jerusalem, El Khudx, 'the holy', seemed very apt. Much had changed since they were last there. Israel was suspended between high tension wires. The 4000-year struggle between Arab and Jew was still simmering.

It was mid-afternoon when a weary group of men checked in at the Jerusalem Towers Hotel. Shabbat had two hours to run. After the fast-moving events of the past 20 hours, sleep engulfed them all and Shabbat was over before they re-entered the world to stroll around the city.

Jerusalem had expanded in all directions. The New City was cleaner and more modern than back in 1971, with museums, the Knesset and many of Jerusalem's restaurants and nightlife. The Old City felt familiar to them, although the restoration of the Jewish quarter had become the most successful building project in Israel.

They strolled in the Arab markets for a while, looking at leather goods and clothes. Steve looked for a small rug for Amanda.

"I've got a feeling we're going to be exchanging presents again," he said simply. That was said with disarming frankness and his companions were warmed by it.

Seven gates were doors into fascinating narrow streets. Climbing the metal staircase on the corner of Habad St, they found themselves on the same level as the rooftops. Through the ventilation shafts, the markets could be seen as well as heard. History seeped into the four men. They could make out Mt Scopus, where the Romans had camped during the siege of Jerusalem. To the east lay the Mount of Olives. The sun was going down. It was clear why Jerusalem was called the City of Gold.

In the Old City, they found a restaurant selling excellent Yemenite falafel. As they ate, little was spoken. They were busy reliving the past. Only a vague itinerary was agreed. By then, it was about nine and they agreed to wander tomorrow towards the Temple Mount. It seemed the right direction to take.

"This is the fulcrum of history," Jack remarked. "Here is where nations have marched." So much had been prophesied, so much had come to its fulfilment.

But as the final curtain was being called on the second Millennium, Jerusalem was at fever-pitch. Even at that time of night, the City was heaving with visitors, bracing itself for a stampede as four million people felt this was the place to be.

They passed by a number of street preachers warning of imminent judgement upon the world. One man was speaking in sober, reasonable tones. Steve and the others found themselves listening, their interest aroused. But on the other side of the street, there was a rather more eccentric figure with flowing robes and a flowing beard. Their taxi companion had wasted no time. They watched as Israeli police descended and took both away. The authorities were taking no chances. The

Jerusalem syndrome was getting out of hand. Some people had only to touch down in Israel to become convinced they were biblical figures vital to world history.

But now the four stood for a while at the Western Wall, remembering the Jewish men they had seen a few hours before, heads covered with cardboard yarmulkas. In the distance, a clock chimed ten. At the Temple Mount, security was tighter than normal. Israel had embarked on a seven-million-pound project to protect the Temple Mount from groups plotting to bring about the end of the world.

Sunday morning dawned over Jerusalem. It was misty.

The four discussed how to connect with the past. They agreed they would walk to the very spot where the bus had been bombed and stand there for a while, though they only had a vague idea of what would or should happen.

Steve meandered round, ignoring the pressing invitation of numerous street traders. "Have a looksie, have a butchers", some said in mocking sales English.

But Steve didn't respond to their bantering tone. He couldn't get out of his mind the face of a wailing woman who stared back at him from the Sahara sands. Steve had always been a survivor, always landed on his feet, always conceived himself to be invincible, possessed of an indestructible quality that gave him mastery of life. Now it bore upon him that life hung by a slender thread. He had never really troubled himself with the lonely questions of existence. "Good grief. We'll be discussing the meaning of life in a minute," he would say disdainfully if a conversation was going deep. "I leave all that to the religious crowd".

But here, in this place, the need to sort out his own mortality was urgent and pressing.

Their route led down Via Dolorosa, spanning both Muslim and Christian quarters. They found themselves amidst a hubbub of priests and pilgrims holding high a crucifix. It took a few minutes to realise the procession they had stumbled into was the traditional route retracing the footsteps of Jesus.

"We could find some other way," Jack called to Steve.

"No let's stay with this," Steve said with a quiet but emphatic voice.

"It does seem to be the most direct route," observed Jack.

"Maybe it'll make it that much more meaningful," Bill wondered.

"Carry on guys," said Liam.

The four men walked on in silence, glancing occasionally at the guide book so they could connect with what had happened long ago. Though the human presence in the hubbub around them was unmistakable, each man felt a silence in his soul as if time was standing still. Strangely, mysteriously, they began to grow unconscious of the crowd. It was becoming powerful, almost overwhelming as their immediate past, 1971 and the events of the crucifixion began to blend together.

One single event and one single moment.

On they walked, immersed in their thoughts, entering the world of lostness inside them that slowly rose up to crack the surface. The throng of people was a river carrying them inexorably into the Church of the Holy Sepulchre. Here was the site where traditionally it had all happened, where six hours of sorrow and pain beyond imagining had reversed the mad course of the world and brought about a vast sweeping arc of redemption that would reconnect the heavens and the earth.

"I'm in darkness," whispered Steve, and in that darkness, he cried out.

But they all felt it, standing there for a while as their lostness rose up within them and their spirits fell and fell into the heavy darkness. Now it was as black as the silence of the empty night before the world began. They had returned to the beginning of all things.

Each of the men in that group was conscious of the pain and sorrow that had shaped their lives but each, too, became acutely conscious of their part in it all, the mad course of the world in which they were eager runners, not just spectators. The atmosphere held them all. A service was proceeding and the Church was filling up.

Without a word, the four withdrew from that place and walked the half-mile or so to where a bus had been ripped apart all those years before.

"I think it was here," said Steve.

Bill and Jack remembered clearly enough. In stark colours, they saw three cowering boys, watching with uncomprehending horror as a voluntary man dissolved before their eyes. They watched as his blood fountained over them.

They heard their own voices mingling their screams with those of the other passengers. They saw the gaping hole arrive unannounced in the back of the bus; they heard again the sirens of police cars and the wails of women. What was there to do? What could they say?

Liam opened himself afresh to the love that had sought him through those years of pain, the compatriot of his sufferings, identifying with the essential solidarity of the world. 'Behold the Man'. How much it had affected him he could not say.

As they thought of the way that fateful day had altered the course of their lives, the men felt as if they had entered into a cave where the dark pain of the world pressed in from every side. Liam did his best to reassure them it wasn't their fault and that they were not responsible. After a while, he gave up trying to assuage their guilt. There was more in the stakes than the incident they were reliving.

"It's the whole of my life that is coming before me!" said Jack. His brother gripped his arm. He felt it too, as together, they returned to the emotions of the scene.

"It is done," Liam said. "We cannot re-write the past but we can be forgiven."

And each of them felt the sweep of their lives pressing in upon them. Slowly, they walked back but paused for a while in the Garden Tomb area. The crowd waters parted and a bench was vacated on which three of them sat. Steve stood to one side.

Now, Bill realised why he couldn't let himself off the hook. It would be tantamount to saying that yes, Sarah had been reduced to a wreckage on the freeway, but there was no further price to pay. It would seem to minimise the way his father had put him down most days. Though long since absent from him, he found himself thinking about old Harry and how things hadn't worked out; the hunter and the hunted. Maybe the old protest against himself could finally be laid to rest.

"I feel my life can start again," said Liam, filled with emotion.

Something was happening. Steve suddenly glimpsed again that time when he had scraped the walls of his house and found old beams that had stood out in their antique wooden beauty. "They've been under your nose all along," said Liam gently.

Bill remembered, once more, those scenes from his childhood when he had seen that estuary dredged of its mud and muck. He felt clean water welling up inside.

"There's been a whispering in your spirit for a long time," Liam said tenderly. Bill knew that he would be taking care of Ali's child and bringing a little life up as if his own. He didn't need to keep on paying the price. Sarah could be given a decent burial. He was let off the hook at last. And Bill broke down and wept as he had not wept for a long time.

Jack felt an unaccountable sense of joy. He had the oddest sensation of holding an armchair to the sky to welcome his guest and of being dazzled by the air. He felt as though he was talking and that someone was listening. "It's time you went through a door of your new house and discovered all those rooms you didn't know were there," said Liam.

Then Jack had an awareness that he was loved wholly and completely. The world had been black and white, but now bright colours adorned the sky. In that moment, Jack knew he would try to find a way of bringing hope to Liz; that new beginnings could drown the wreckage of the old world that had passed its sell-by date. Engulfed with emotion, Steve went to him; Joseph and his brothers were reconciled.

A lump rose within everyone present and broke like a wave breaks upon a shoreline. For an hour, the wetness of weary tears swept over them and they talked and prayed. All, in some way, felt that their lives had been redeemed. It was time to go.

The next few weeks were heavy with the sound of pages turning. Chapters yet to be written were invested with a new plot. That was a new beginning. But, like all new beginnings, there was an original beginning; and a beginning beyond that.

Chapter Two:

Tonight We Saw a Pink Moon

Moonrise that night was larger than usual. A bright glow was cast on the horizon of the chimneys. Our neighbour looked bigger, brighter, nearer. It didn't usually get this close.

"So why do they call it pink?" asked Katie, mesmerised by the eerie glow that wrapped enchantment round the Moon. They had watched in the garden, fascinated, as the moon climbed higher, assuming a brilliance and a sharpness that brought its craters within reach of their hands.

"It's named after an early-blooming wildflower in North America," explained her father. "Pretty good, isn't it?"

"Breathtaking!" said Katie. "It gives such a sense of calm and positivity over everything. Just makes you peaceful to look at it. Don't think I've seen it this big!"

Planet Earth was shutting down fast. Everyone had to shun society. Across the globe, Governments rushed to impose draconian controls over their people that had never been seen before. We were living through mass quarantine. There were a few lunatics spoiling things for everyone else but tonight was the global fellowship of lunar admirers. Across the world, people were looking at the Supermoon, pausing from prison to glance upwards and take in the view. Well-known landmarks were being photographed against its radiating glow. Though separated from each other by fences and shuttered lock-down, fellow-watchers were joined in solidarity. The little piece of flotsam and jetsam they called Covid-19 had come together to catch on to unsuspecting humanity with virulent force. It had taken down cities, systems, communities and communities of systems. People and families had been overwhelmed. The sound of weeping and wailing had gone up from countless homes – yet here was the Moon, steady and serene, making its regular call from the Sea of Tranquillity.

"Don't think I've paid such attention to the moon before," Katie remarked after a while. It was then that she saw him. Across the street stood a youngish man, watching the night sky in rapt attention. 'I don't think I've seen him before either,' she thought to herself. It was if the thought had willed itself into wings. He averted his gaze suddenly and looked across the street. Eyes met and then smiles coalesced. A wave followed. He seemed to be alone but went in after a few minutes.

"Who's that?" Katie asked her father.

"Oh, that's Robert Morrison," said Bill. "He moved in eighteen months ago after his wife died in a car accident. Think he came to have a change of scenery. Previous place too full of memories, I suppose."

Bill knew about that and imagination filled in the gaps.

Through the atmosphere of his aching and often cloudy soul, the astronomer in him caught fire, though with a subdued wet flame. What would it be like, he wondered as he had so many times before, to stand on the edge of the universe to gaze into the unknown and uncharted? The estate just went on and on. Before their last walk together, Bill and his wife Sarah had to move quickly along a California beach or they would have been cut off by the tides; as if Earth was being rocked by the Moon and water sloshed about helplessly. The human footprints still on the Sea of Tranquillity were embedded deeply in the imagination of his boyhood. That was before the troubles arose and his own tranquillity was forever raped. The events in Jerusalem, the loss of his mother, Micky in Vietnam, Sarah and now this. The rush of tragic memories moved quickly past him.

'Why is the world in such a hurry?' he thought. 'Ever since we have been born, we've been space travellers; living on a world constantly rotating, spinning and turning on a non-stop journey. Does the universe listen to the ache in my heart?' his inner soul cried out as he strained to hear. Was there a friendly face behind everything? Could he put a name to the face?

"We are a sophisticated generation, used to computers, space probes and discerning between the images of Hollywood," he had often reasoned. "Is there anything out there that corresponds to what is in here?" Bill's inner voice had cried indignantly.

After a while, he walked back to an empty house, silent with the intensity that clothes the hours of the night. Katie joined him. She had found herself wondering if Robert Morrison was going to put in another appearance. About to dismiss herself as a lunatic, there he was again; again the wave.

She wondered if she should wander over but thought it wasn't really allowed.

"You're in very pensive mood, Dad," she said.

Bill had been seated for a while, giving only perfunctory responses to comments and questions. Time past had raced at blurring speed but now one particular period of months had dragged themselves by. Katie wondered about the letters and documents she had been allowed to read.

"Who is this Liam?" she asked. "His name seems to come up a lot."

It took a minute for the trance fog of memories to dissipate. Bill Trimble was playing host to his guest from the UK back near the turn of the Millennium. An internet dialogue had led to an invitation to come out to California. Liam was taking some seminars and speaking across the West coast of the US about spirituality. He was a lecturer in microbiology at a college on the outskirts of London and often spoke at meetings, but had recently begun to accept wider engagements outside of term-time. He was a deep thinker; wanted to be a Vicar. Now Bill told Katie of this.

"When we met for the first time and took the measure of each other, there was a worn, almost hungry look about him as if he needed taking in hand. Meeting Liam had the ring of significance."

They had driven through steep twisting streets that wound through overgrown hills north of the University where Bill had a weekday apartment. Within two hours, they were descending the foothills again to enter the gourmet ghetto boasting restaurants renowned throughout San Francisco Bay. They made for Chez Panisse, home to the California Cuisine. Bill's cell phone went but it wasn't her. A hidden emotion was working its way up to the surface. Bill's whole face moved. Where was Ali? Why had there been no more contact?

"How did your people come to America?" Liam had asked Bill over dinner, hungry for leads and confirmation. Suddenly, a fixed stare had held Bill and he dropped his eyes. He had told a few people that his close friend Ali had AIDS. Was that why she cut off contact after a few faltering steps when she had renewed contact after a discomforting break? It merged in his mind with Mum's illness.

"My grandfather was a boy of three when the family fled the pogroms of Czarist Russia," Bill replied. "They were numbered among a million who arrived in America in the year 1905 to build a new life."

A friendly smile never left Bill's face but there seemed to be a masked, petulant sadness.

"Did they come straight to California?" Liam had enquired.

Bill narrowed his eyes. "No, that happened after the crash of 1929 when there weren't any jobs back east. Josef Petrovsky, Grandpa on my mother's side, joined the despairing ranks of sixteen million unemployed. Like so many, he travelled the long dusty road to California: California, the golden land where the streets had money on the ground, " Bill had remarked sardonically. But here was Katie.

"Grandma Petrovsky died in the last global pandemic," he told her.

"You mean Spanish flu?" she asked.

"That's what they called it," replied Bill. "It wasn't actually Viva L'Espagne. They only called it that back in 1918 as there was a concentration in Madrid as there is at the moment. It's what we do best – blame foreigners, just like at the moment: Kung Flu, the Chinese virus."

"Yes," agreed Katie. They had both seen the news that night after the daily Government Briefing.

"I think when they tried to do some source-tracing, the culprit was a poultry farm in Kansas," Bill said. "It jumped the species barrier and before you knew it, millions were coughing their lungs out. A neighbour along the street told me once that her grandmother had lost her fiancé through that. I grew up on war-gaming and military history but you could read about the titanic battles of 1918 without any realisation that a pandemic was leaping along the trenches of friend and foe alike."

Katie shook her head in sadness. She looked at Bill. She knew he wasn't her real father. Her mother's boyfriend – well, that had been good enough for her these twenty years. They were close.

Bill told Katie that his grandfather found menial work at first at the observatory on Mt Wilson, north-west of Los Angeles. The family interest in space began. Those were exciting times to be at Mt Wilson, in whatever capacity. The new 100-inch telescope was yielding a dramatic view of the universe. The astronomy bug was highly contagious. In the second generation, Bill's uncle caught it. He worked his way through college, applied for and got a job at the silver-domed 200-inch telescope on Mt Palomar when it opened in '48. With unparalleled ability to gather light, the observatory unveiled a universe twice as big as anyone had thought. The Moon was only 8 miles away.

Bill went on with his story with Katie.

"That's where I come into the story," he said. "It was a good time for us at first. The memory of those days in Britain now seems painted with sunlight. I went to a private school near Brighton. It meant I was separated from my parents during term-time. "

"Many of the kids made fun of my stutter," Bill continued. "But I guess I was blessed with mum's capacity for making friends. It served me well till she died."

A dim, diffused softness filled Bill's voice before he regained composure. "No one was surprised that I followed in the family tradition. I guess a liberal helping of stardust had been sprinkled in my eyes too," he chuckled. "I went out there myself after getting my doctorate to do research at Berkeley."

"Did your grandfather have faith?" Katie suddenly asked.

"Yes, he certainly did." Bill was surprised at the question as he was unaware he had ever discussed that with Katie.

"Think I found a reference to that in one of the letters," she answered.

"Well, I'll tell you," said Bill. "It never caught on for me, especially after we lost Mum. After Jerusalem, it had begun to make sense though, at least the second time. The gaping years were done."

"You mean it made sense for the second time?" puzzled Katie.

"The second visit," Bill said. "It bridged the gap between what's inside here and what's out there."

Katie disappeared to write some emails. Bill sat there travelling across time and space, faster than light-speed.

He had found himself getting on well with Liam, his new friend. Across the bay, lights illuminated the city. Outside Bill's home, a large shed housed a 20-inch telescope. With little cloud cover to impede viewing and away from the glare of San Francisco, Liam was able to peer into space. His host provided expert commentary.

"Our galaxy is not alone," Bill had explained. "No corner of the night sky is exempt from those pinpricks. We only saw so much with the naked eye. Even with the early telescopes, we were unsure what those faint wisps were between the stars."

"But then," he said with incredulity, "we found they were distant worlds, other galaxies! Andromeda, our neighbour, is also a rotating mass of millions of stars!"

Through a telescope, the only galaxy that could be seen unaided exploded into cosmic beauty. Bill paused before starting up again.

"Everywhere we look, the place is teeming with galaxies. 70 billion galaxies! Who knows how many more? The number keeps rising the further we look."

Bill had been unable to contain himself as he said this and Liam heard cosmic music play. To join that song was to begin to understand. Bill told him about his grandfather, who comforted him after the gaping years when Mum died and Dad had been unable to handle life for a while.

"Tell me about the stars, Grandpa," Bill would plead as they plied the river in search of breakfast.

"Those were exciting times!" his grandfather had replied, warmed by soft nostalgic light. His eyes lit up in sparkling reminiscence. The air itself had been alive as the dimensions of the cosmic architecture began to grip everyone who worked at Mt Wilson. Together, they had set out to chart the night sky.

"And then," Bill had exclaimed to Liam, "the chief at Mt Wilson, Edwin Hubble, proposed that our Milky Way is part of a vast scheme with no special place and no privileged position. What's more, we're still on the move, accelerating every second. Suddenly, the size of the universe had leapt by 1000 million. It's what they call dark energy, a mysterious force pushing everything apart."

Bill had looked down and his voice lowered as if he was about to convey the secret of the universe. Between sips of coffee, they tucked into a fruitcake Bill brought out from somewhere as the evening turned into small hours.

"Think of it!" he exclaimed. "It's growing. It's getting bigger. Stars are moving away from each other just like these currants baked in the oven. Every other currant is moving further apart too! If the stars are shooting away at such a colossal rate, the universe must be expanding. Fast!"

"I just can't take this in," Liam had said, whistling softly. "I read somewhere that astronomers now think the universe is growing even faster than we suspected. And what about black holes?"

"Everyone wants to know about these celestial monsters from which no light can escape," said Bill, the astronomer, smiling.

"It was just theory at first," he said. "Surely something would prevent so bizarre an object from actually existing? But observations are mounting up to show that these strangest of objects in the universe are for real."

"Any near us?" Liam had asked. He suddenly felt like a tourist.

"Our local black hole may be only 10,000 light-years away in the constellation of Cygnus," Bill Trimble replied. "We're beginning to detect such monsters as rotating black holes that drag space and time round like a tornado. Heard about a Millennium sport? Planet-hunting in other solar systems?"

Now, his voice trembled with awe. "You know, it's curious," he said. "The more we find out, the more we retreat in amazement. The cosmos has not stopped pulling surprises on us. People have looked up and thought they had it all worked out. And then some new observation bombed complacency, until today, we stand numb and in shock. Just how big is it? How much more is there?"

"As many stars in the sky as there are grains of sand on the seashore," said Liam, quoting the Bible.

"I reckon that's about right," Bill had replied. But even as he said that, he was back on a beach near to where he went to school in Britain, where he used to stand watching the dredgers scooping muck and mud from the bottom of the estuary. After the shock of losing Sarah, he had just been beginning to feel that if only he could let go of the past, a vigorous, purposeful life would be given to him.

Two days later, Ali had come down the lonely drive and the roof had blown off.

That was then. For now, Bill thought he would write to Liam. It had been a while. Katie had said everyone needed to reach out to friends old and new in order to conserve and expand. That had to include friends who had helped sort out your mortality.

Dear Liam,

I thought I would write to see how you are doing in a Covid world? Assume you are self-isolating like most of us.

What a weird time we live in! The collateral damage to society and the economy is going to be huge.

This lockdown has given us lots of time for self-reflection. The pace of life is slower now. News keeps infiltrating the whole time like an unwelcome intruder. Only the important things are important now and the small things don't seem to matter. In time, this will pass for us all and the light around will shine much brighter than it did before. Katie is amazing and I'm lucky to be in a safe environment with her. Her flat sale being delayed has taken a while which has worked out really well. Katie's best friend Maddy is a nurse and doesn't, in any case, have a relationship with either of her parents where going back would be an option. That's really sad. Maybe we should invite her to live here but we can't. You will know, I expect, that Eyam in Derbyshire quarantined itself during the Black Death. And there they stayed until it was all over. Everywhere, borders have closed and nations have shut themselves in. This is a world where shutters are down. How do we inhabit those broader places where we used to live, that beckon to us like the memory of another world we had left behind, receding into the horizon?

Home is a weird place for me because it reminds me of when my mental health was really bad a few years ago. You helped me find faith twenty years back and that's really helping.

It's ridiculous. Why do we kid ourselves that we should feature at all when we hardly loom very high in the scheme of things? Maybe we are only the sigh of the universe yet none of us can live like that.

Tonight, we saw a Pink Moon. Did you see it from wherever? In fact, not sure where you are at the moment. You always were a guru sort of person, so interested to know what you are making of it all? I thought tonight about that evening we spent in San Francisco peering through the telescope in my shed. We were awed. That night, we talked for hours, our conversation interrupted but also stimulated by peering through the eyepiece. Coffee, like the very universe itself, went on forever. The night sky had put on a stellar performance.....

I recall the words of an old Zen Buddhist poem. "The world is dew... and yet... and yet". How can the spirit keep intact in a place where everything is evaporated as the dew of morning? In the scheme of things, we carry no futile importance. To be involved with ourselves in this way is to add delusion to collusion. Better if we did not feature so highly in our imaginary world and shrank away to a dot on the landscape. And yet... what you taught me those years ago is that we matter to God. And to each other. Until then, it had felt like the old life was going to be shipwrecked. Old patterns would not work for much longer though I would cling to them as long as possible. How things changed for me.

A couple of years before we met, the Leo and Kate Titanic story was about the travails of individuals – the private story. Bit of a contrast between that and that 'Night to Remember' film. Did you ever see it? 1957, I think it was. It was about public safety. So, the private had trumped the public. Where will it go now, though, in this disaster movie? Maybe we'll re-discover what's important.

The story of this crisis can go one of two ways. It can be about being under house arrest, loneliness, of stockpiling and looking after number one. And as ever, it's people in poverty who pay most. Or we can shift into something more hopeful.

How's your family? Your Mum, step-dad Hugh? Do write to me. Hope to hear from you. Bill Trimble

Chapter Three:

They Seek for the Wise

A key turned in the lock of the unremarkable bungalow.

Katie wondered where her Dad was. She called out. Then she saw him, sitting on the decking outside, staring vacantly into the garden.

Bill was lost in reverie. The years had raced backwards, pursued indelicately by time. It was over twenty years ago. In a quiet room in a lunch-hour discussion, over 20 people had gathered during the lunch-break; an assembled group of those whose time to draw breath was shrinking and whose lives were furious wheels, scarcely able to stop. Liam was speaking. He was being seen as a sort of guru.

Liam reminded them that they were made for 24 hours to a day, seven days to a week.

"Have a day of rest. You can't do everything. Sort out priorities. As the Book says, 'Whatever your hand finds to do, do it well'. But be sure to include time for reflection and prayer. Step off the pedal. Be more laid back. Take regular exercise. Take time for people. Neglect of relationships is a sign of burn-out. Make space for music or for reading to nurture your weary soul. Find somewhere, anywhere, those times when you can slow right down in protest against a world that's speeding up."

Katie jumped into the scene. "You ok, Dad?" she asked.

"Hi love," Bill said, turning to her. "I was lost there for a minute."

"Obviously!" Katie replies. "Been happening a lot recently: it's like you're troubled by the ghosts of Christmas past."

Bill told her he had been thinking about a meeting he had been to with his friend Liam. Must have been 1998. They sat down with a cup of tea.

"What's the mood like at school?" he asked Katie.

"It's grim out there," she said. "We're trying to keep things going at the school but it's not easy. Bear in mind that we're only getting twenty-seven at the moment," Katie replied. "That's the offspring of key workers, of course."

"Yes, but how many kids are doing online lessons?" Bill is curious.

"Oh, I don't know," Katie replied. "About ten per cent overall, I should say. In my case, I do these lessons and post them and all that, but it requires the young people to login and do the material. If not, doesn't work."

"Sure," agreed Bill, shrugging his shoulders. "This'll be a wasted year for many. Who knows what the effect will be on their education? Expect they'll repeat."

"But look," he added, "what about those on free school meals?"

"Big problem!" Katie observed. "It's an essential lifeline of support for these families. The poorest families are hit hardest. It's all right for you and I with at least some money coming through and a bungalow with a garden. If your job is precarious, housing is unsuitable or health is tricky, how you going to cope?

One of our Mums is tearing her hair out," Katie went on. "It's like she's imprisoned with her abuser. And it's a tough world out there with her children at home all the time. There are families with nothing, who rely on this money to feed their children," she exclaimed. "We are now delivering food parcels to those who have told us they have nothing to eat.

It's not all bad," Katie added. "Lots of children at the school seem to be enjoying staying home and learning to cook with Mum or Dad."

"This is a savage time," said Bill. "Plenty in the wider world without any safety net of course. "Yes, indeed," said Katie, finishing her tea. "The UN warned today that the world is at risk of widespread famines of biblical proportions caused by the pandemic."

Bill shook his head. What was there to say?

"Not a lot," said Katie. "But speaking of food, don't want you to feel guilty or anything but I think it's my turn to get supper, Dad," Katie exclaimed. She wandered out to the kitchen and poured a drink. She pressed the button on her MP3. It was her favourite song. *"Some people would say to accept their fate. Well if this is fate then we'll find a way to cheat,"* Starley sings. *"You know you can call on me, if you can't stop the tears from falling down."* Katie joined in as she cut some broccoli. *"If the cavalry and the help don't come, well then we'll find a way to dodge the smoking gun."*

Her phone pinged. There was a text from her friend Maddy, training to be a nurse. She's been called up.

"Seen that guy over the road again?" Bill asked suddenly. He was standing in the doorway.

"What guy is that?" said Katie, a little too nonchalantly.

"Robert Morrison, as I'm sure you know!" Bill smiles.

"Oh, him," said Katie. "We had a little exchange yesterday morning as I got into my car just as he was doing the same. He said he's on the neighbourhood What's App group. We'll probably meet later."

"Great!" said Bill. He was glad for her to get out and meet people even if it meant staying in. Anybody would be an improvement over Freddie.

He was very glad that they had been able to fit in that trip to South Africa. Bill had looked up old friends, they had done some sightseeing and been able to visit Katie's Grandmother, Miriam, who lived in Soweto.

Once upon a time in Soweto....

Once upon a time in Soweto, everyone who was politically inclined was labelled a Communist. It was a shanty town slum in those days. Not far away, well-watered people relaxed in well-watered gardens. They were the whites. Like Bill's Aunt Frances.

Then there were those who inhabited corrugated-iron shacks. They were the blacks or the coloureds, who lived amongst dirty, dusty, unlit streets, out of sight and out of mind. When they had performed their daily service for their masters, they stepped back into the shadows of invisibility in enclaves provided. Like Miriam, for instance. She had gone to live in the US but now she felt ready to leave her California existence and re-connect with the suburbs of Johannesburg where she had lived amidst the hard racism of Apartheid days.

Liam's work as a mediator had brought him here several times before, to bring people together who wanted to knock old walls down. This was a different type of encounter. Bill's cousin Frances had lost her mother in the surge of violence and pain before the birth of the new South Africa. It was the last straw for the family. There had been no one to hit out at, no one who could move out of the shadows of history with a name or a face upon whom she could pin this shattering event that still shook her from top to bottom. But now, Frances had returned to visit friends.

South West Townships, or Soweto as it was once called, was a pastiche of tiny tin-roofed homes as far as the eye could see; a litter-strewn landscape. In the Apartheid era, the Government had crushed the squatter communities into a mass of shanty towns; council bungalows with two rooms, an outside toilet and a standpipe for water.

Miriam greeted them in her modernised bungalow. Though not on a par with Frances' house, which she had visited often where her mother worked as a maid, she was proud of the mains drains, water on tap and electricity to power their homes such as the whites had enjoyed for years. She and Katie embraced. They spoke for a while about the past.

Bill said that when Miriam came to the house Frances occupied in order to clean, Frances was aware what a very different experience Miriam would have had. White families had their gated enclave but black kids often scrambled amongst the refuse.

"It's true," concurred Miriam with anger and sadness in her voice. "The prize was a school meal provided by the State that had been discarded by you white kids in favour of a lunch box from Mum. School meals for black and coloured children had been banned by Dr Verwoerd. If we can't feed all non-white kids, we can't feed any!"

Miriam showed Katie some old photos. They were of that day in June '76. The children of Soweto took to the streets in a mass protest against Bantu education and the use of Afrikaans, the language of the oppressor, as the language of instruction. Singing, they marched from school to school.

"You can't see me amongst the 15,000 but I'm somewhere in the crowd," said Miriam.

The police responded brutally. The world saw pictures of singing children facing attack - dogs and armed police. Six hundred died. But there came a time when the humiliating self-doubt of the black population rose up with indignation and determination. 'Black consciousness', they called it.

"I can't think how we all accepted it," Frances often told Bill. "The pretence was that keeping the races apart would allow for healthy separation. But humans find it enormously difficult to treat differences as equal. They have to go in for grading. Light-skinned people are superior. It's how things are, or so we thought. How could I have downloaded such a programme? To me, it was so normal."

"What happened to your mother? I heard later that she had died," Bill asked Miriam.

Miriam hesitated. And under the enquiring eyes and warmth of invitation, the river started to flow about the day her father greeted her with a face such as she had never seen him wear before. Katie listened with total concentration and then began to ask questions.

Bill left them to it, saluting their courageous conversation. Soweto was not the same as when Miriam roamed these streets in the days of her childhood. Now there were shopping - malls, cinemas, a golf course, a university and the biggest hospital in Africa; altogether a place for the new black middle to stay rather than migrate to the old white suburbs. He wandered down the street where two Nobel Laureates had once lived. At the entrance to the Apartheid Museum were seven concrete columns, each engraved with a cornerstone of the 1994 Constitution. Democracy, equality, reconciliation, diversity, responsibility, respect, freedom: it was the most liberal constitution ever, in theory!

He went in, struck by white concrete blocks and yellow rubble from the goldmines, past green wooden benches with the words "whites only" etched on them and the dreaded passbook. It was the instrument of humiliation blacks and coloureds had to show whenever the mood crossed a policeman's face. Frances could go anywhere. No place was fenced off. Beaches, parks and toilets were free. Her family didn't have to produce the passbook except at election times to show they could vote. Not for them the infamous pencil test. If a pencil was inserted into your hair and remained, it showed you had frizzy strands and therefore you were definitely non-white.

Words from Mandela were etched onto a granite slab - "*To be free is not merely to cast off one's chains but to live in a way that respects and enhances the freedom of others.*"

It was a lesson Bill and Katie would often discuss. It had become a reference point for them. Katie burned with a mounting sense of injustice. She would become an activist one day.

———————————————

Hello, Bill! It was Liam. What a wonderful surprise! Was only thinking about you the other day!

And how are you doing? Still doing those research papers and travelling? Sorry – forget that last remark! A tad insensitive- of course, you are grounded like everybody else. Having to share a kitchen table to put your laptop? You still in the south of England? Who's at home there with you?

Expect like me you wonder what is happening to all those who can't stay home because they don't have one – like the gent who camps out in our local churchyard at night here in London.

I've just been outside and had a great time going like the clappers! That's the neighbours, by the way, and it's the highlight of our week to cheer and bang saucepans for the health workers. My Dad used to teach history, as you know, and think he would have called them the Spitfire pilots of our time. Generally, I think that we are not seeing other people so we are less connected in one way. But we're definitely more connected through love and we're thinking more about everyone else now.

This is so making us realise our own limitations. Some will find that strength on their own but I suspect most of us are obliged to reach out to some other source to meet the challenge. If we have learned anything it is that kindness counts. It was Plato who said that we should be kind to all because everyone is fighting a hard battle. Now that's the kind of quote you think is in the Bible!

Speaking of which, I'm doing another version of vicaring: peace and reconciliation work.

A movement of the brave, a glimpse of a people's alliance is where it all began for me - a glint in the eye holding me in remorseless focus, sapping all other energies except towards the goal. We don't want schemers: we need dreamers.

A goal, did I say? No, that cannot be it. That is too mechanical, too technocratic. A dream would be more accurate; a vision asking, 'Why not?' You said once that a global consensus could never come about, even for successful dreamers, even for pragmatic dreamers who combine what they see in the night with a healthy grasp of the possible. Nevertheless, possibility is transforming the world for me, and I continue in my journey (electronically now) with the same sense of adventure that we shared all those years ago. And yes, I am keenly aware of the wretched ambiguity this evokes.

I endeavour to help neighbours, families and groups in dispute to learn to value each other so as to be open to each other's narratives. Maybe this will extend to a broader canvas in time. As Napoleon remarked, "Victory belongs to the most persevering!"

So many I know seem to take refuge in rationalisations which are so bland people have stopped listening to them. What wisdom and strength do the politicians convey to be shepherds or maybe fathers and mothers to their people? I tell you: it would be good to think there is a spiritual turning at long last. We yearn to find a vision we can hold on to carry us forward. Maybe now voices can be heard. This time we want to listen to those voices and The Voice: perhaps.

Until we all had to experience mass incarceration, wherever I went and I got together with people over a drink or a meal, the conversation turned to the subterranean issues of life, the inner vision without which we are wandering listlessly in the dark. It's like there's a hunger that can only be acknowledged in whispers, a hunger to be heard and to matter, somehow, amidst a universe that belies our significance. It's ridiculous. Why do we kid ourselves that we should feature at all when we hardly loom very high in the scheme of things? Maybe we are only the sigh of the universe.

The landscape of the mind is, after all, a site of ambiguity when it comes to our having any value. Some experience of being written off may be necessary to spur ourselves on or for human creativity. It was Nietzsche who said, "I say unto you, a man must have chaos yet within him to give birth to a dancing star." Undeniably though, put-downs can be amusing at times. My favourite is Samuel Johnson who said of Milton's 'Paradise Lost', that it was a book easy to put down - hard to pick up!

I don't have all the answers. I'm still learning. What I do have is questions. And I ask plenty of questions, to enquire what people are really thinking about their underlying concerns. Aunt Miriam helped me to recover when I hit the buffers just as I did when Dad died. She casts her own particular brand of magic, turning her weaving into a metaphor for life. Her love of music was also pressed into service. She was intriguing.

"Listen to the music," she said. "Tune in to the themes playing deep down. And as the songs are heard, they will change in the hearing just as stories evolve in the telling."

When the Covid asteroid fell to earth, I made all these resolutions. I joined dozens of social networks advising me how to spend my new-found free time, looked online for some great physical fitness training and decided I would speak and cook Italian like a native. I remembered the other day a meal I had out in California with Steve, not long after we met. For once, Steve was talking openly about the deeper questions of life. He was surprised at himself. Animated conversation led to lunch.

"You like Italian?" asked Steve. "Fine by me!"

I remember looking intently at this man with jet-black hair that toned in with his skin colouring and a dark blue shirt. "So, is the human mind as fast as a computer?" I asked, as we sat waiting for the deep-fried pizza. Picture the scene. A weathered, auburn- haired woman was approaching, clutching a tray as she picked her way through a crowded restaurant. "About a million nerve endings from your eye to the brain have just worked simultaneously to build that picture," Steve told me. "It's stunning. In your brain, there are as many neurons as there are stars in the galaxy. An average neuron has tens of thousands of inputs and outputs. The old transistors we used when I began had only a few." He knew about all that, of course, as he was CEO of a Silicon Valley start-up before he took it back to UK.

In the light of what happened subsequently, I had glanced at Steve, yielding to a deeper place of memory and encounter and power-driven emotions. It was definitely him. The youth and magic of that morning had suddenly become an evening grown weary with the past. I tried to compose myself by reaching down to the place of inward refreshing to which I was no stranger. Years after Dad's death, Aunt Miriam had shown me where it was. "How's life treating you?" was all I could muster, though it struck me as being trifling and fumbling, utterly incapable of doing justice to the encounter. Conversation ranged briefly across continents, time zones and families.

I have no idea why I am telling you this except as a round-about way of saying I am still in touch with Steve and his half-brother Jack. These days I seem to have an unstoppable online social life – on Messenger, WhatsApp, Skype and, of course, the ubiquitous Zoom. Whoever had shares in that made a smart move. But there was Steve. And there was Jack! It occurs to me I could fix up a Zoom drink together if you'd like that?

Talk soon.

Liam

Dear Liam,

What a fabulously informative and reflective email! Wasn't expecting all that but why am I surprised?

I'm doing ok though feeling for all those who are confined to some pretty small barracks or trapped with an abusive partner! If nothing else, this is an opportunity all ways round to make some big changes. Fear is forcing us into realising our interconnectedness and dependency beyond ourselves.

It's interesting how nourishing your own space and taking care of yourself has gone from nice-to-have indulgence to must-have necessity. As this is the biggest existential moment in our lifetime, rarely has it been so universally pressing. What are you doing to service yourself as well as clearly reaching out to others and helping us think? It's so fresh to hear bird song rather than the sound of cars outside. Apart from social distancing and putting a human shield round health systems in case they get overwhelmed, we can't do much about Covid. But we can control exercise, diet, sleep and enjoy the reward of calling old friends like you. Many of my pals have Zoom calls with colleagues, so it's great to harness the power of telecommunications to stay in touch with everyone. Think it was Aristotle who said, without friends, we would not choose to live though we had all other goods?

Getting creative? They say a good book restores your vision of life. We absolutely have to develop the potential of people everywhere as we come through this crisis situation. Our big resource is people and the scope for creative optimism and practical solutions. Just hope the children at Katie's school will understand that.

At the same time, though, as we absolutely need to be realistic about the present time and be optimistic about the future, do you think there's a place to be gentle with our past – or nostalgic?

There is no precedence in living memory for any of this. Bang goes our predictable lives. Maybe unpredictability is the nature of things, contingency by another word, and assured security is the exception. Yet how do you do life with that? Farmers have to sow seeds knowing harvest will come!

Yes, would love to have a reunion with Steve and Jack. What are they doing with themselves?

Take care,

Bill

Hi Bill,

What an interesting series of points you make! Lots of food for thought. In the meantime, how the world's poor get physical food security at the moment is incredibly disturbing. This cunning virus is shining a harsh light on the profound inequalities that scar the globe like the Rift Valley in Africa.

It would be such a missed opportunity if rich countries work their way to get back to normal but those 'normal' patterns of how things are done leave poorer areas unable to deal with ravages. 'Normal' wasn't such a good place to be. The future can be kinder than the past.

Crisis won't change our egoism but it does show what the common good is for the benefits we all need. We need a New Deal to come out of this and not just think in terms of narrow nationalism. Inclusivity and an economy that deals with a public good agenda are essential. It is the personal attention and care tailor-made by health workers rather than structured for everyone that is taking care of people at the time. The plates are shifting. We'll have to get past the international blame game, though. That is definitely not showing us in a good light. Just think of this, though. Futures are usually created by the high-powered elites. Maybe we could alter that so it's not just top-down.

Busy trying to figure out how we can give birth to a new way of being the church so as to be a lot more responsive to the world's needs and not just ensuring our own survival. Solidarity, racial justice, a fair deal for marginalised groups, those big inequalities and the existential threat of climate change is as least as important as tradition.

It used to feel like another universe to try to discern a global consensus standing up for the care of people and the value of the world where we are embedded - those con-joined twins. But it would be helpful to use you as a sounding board for the thoughts and ideas that have been building up for a while. Let me know if that would be ok. I'm getting more and more convinced that you just can't understand the interior landscape without some concept of the struggle to realise our sense of inner worth and what I call 'a valuable self'. So how do you do a trade-off between lives and the economy?

Nostalgic about the past? That's a tough one. When Dad died, Mum married Hugh and we all moved to Belfast. Such certainties as I possessed were now as ephemeral as a lingering puff from a steam train; imposing one minute, then gone with the wind. From that time, Hugh worked overtime to make us fit in with his previous family. It keeps coming back to me how insistently he would urge upon us the only ethic he knew - "We can't have anybody around who is not one of us. You can do whatever you want. You'll go far. Build up a head of steam. No one can stop you. Show them all what you can do, whose son you are!"

It was dinned into me, morning, noon and night. My most enduring memory is that of a rather fat, bald figure puffing out his chest in a red armchair by the fire, sitting back in a haze of self-satisfaction and congratulation. I guess he had reason. His business was growing quickly. Then came Sundays and he would take us to church; one more opportunity to breathe out pleasure in his achievements.

At the risk of putting an emotional burden on an old man, now deceased, the sarcasm and the put-downs were arrows Hugh used to devastating effect. I doubt if it came from serving in the Army but he was a skilled verbal archer. An arrow? Don't mean that. To me, it felt more like he was an axe-wielding warrior when he got going.

Don't know if I shared with you that day Hugh passed away. It was heart-rending to hear Mum wishing she had gone to see him earlier that afternoon as she often did; if only she had a memory of holding his hand. Those dark, grief-lined eyes! None of us knew what to say or do, though this was hardly an unfamiliar landscape. The mascara on her face was lined with tears like river valleys.

I was glad I was there and made the first move as we embraced and the tears flowed. For years, Mum had waited for this moment but both she and Hugh had put up too many barriers.

Now, all the planned words dissolved. As we were never able to see Dad like that, it was really poignant to see my step-father with calm on his face that lent him an air of gentleness, rarely expressed in life.

In those last few months, Hugh knew he didn't have long. Yet, I was struck as I always am by the tenacity of the human spirit and a defiant unwillingness to be resigned to the inevitable. It is what I am coming to call, "The Protest". The narcissism of self-importance as Freud characterised it? Or was it the sigh of "I count .... I matter?"

From where I sat, I never felt I measured up, that Hugh was indifferent to me. That feeling was a ghost which he had commanded to walk the painful corridors of my mind. Until recently, I cursed myself because he knew I still craved for recognition from a father-figure - but let's call him for what he is: my step-father, now old and frail. Some years on, the ghost had finally stopped walking. I needed to make my peace with him before he died. He held out this limp handshake. At first, it wasn't easy for me to take. What did I want with a limp hand? Afterwards, I was pleased I had.

I stepped out of the room and was glad to take in a little of the atmosphere of the nursing home where Hugh spent his last days. It was certainly not clad with any sense of impending doom. Rather, it was dominated by a lively group of old folk who had formed a cabal against death. After a late supper, a few old records had filled the room with the light and colour of nostalgia at its best. There had been some merriment and they were having a cup of hot chocolate. Matron cleared their cups away, a lady who breathed out an atmosphere of kindness and reassurance in the way she treated them with dignity, unlike some nurses who keep asking you the same question. She left them to it. A few of the staff casually joined in the songs as they breezed in and out of the room.

I watched for a few minutes as, in the dying hours of a December night, eight octogenarians exchanged their bittersweet memories of life. They were evidently protective of each other; their solidarity shining through in a brief encounter with someone who had just lost her husband. Their talk was of the times they had lived through that were now drawing to a close. They had seen three new generations. Scattered survivors of their own generation lived on. The darker side of optimism when their parents were alive had been a fin de siècle era of decadence and a relentless search for anything that was new.

The cabal exchanged memories about where and when they were born, discussing what life had been like for them in those alien days when they lived on another planet. It was all there, so vivid; the day before yesterday. The flowering of childhood and adolescent years must have felt like the smell of awakening spring. I doubt if you and I would have felt like that after what happened.

Just then, Mum called me back to outside Hugh's room to discuss funeral plans.

Guess all this is on my mind as I think about how we work our way through the loss of income, family and friends into a more hopeful future. Low-wage sectors are doing the heavy lifting right now and being put under more strain than ever. We're all called to fight a national battle as well as a human crisis. You mentioned Katie's nurse friend, Maddy. Most of us probably know someone who works for the NHS. The coronavirus pandemic is taking a heavy toll on the healthcare workers around the world battling to contain it. Yet, hunkered down as we are though into our national spaces, we don't appreciate that many African countries have hardly any ventilators.

As I say, I don't have all the answers. I'm still learning. What I do have is questions: lots of them. It was Milton Friedman who said it is only a crisis that produces real change but that always depends on the resources of ideas and people that are lying around at any one time. The creation of something else is possible, like seeing those struggling to make ends meet as not because it's their own fault, but as a threat to us all. Pandemics force people to change their world. Different futures are being assembled as we speak, courtesy of technology. At least for now, rates of pollution have come down. And the wealth of billionaires has fallen by a third or so. Poor people have little to lose.

In the meantime, here we are transformed into a walking, talking bubble who might infect others. We can't live life in our own bubble, though, for long. It's all those people who avoid you as if you've got the plague – which, if you think about it, possibly I do! With that, I am off out for daily exercise.

Always remember, Bill, it is better to light a candle than to curse the darkness. Talk soon and I'll see if I can get Steve and Jack together for reunion. You still in touch with Beth? Best not include her, eh?

Liam

PS – A final thought. 'All of humanity's problems stem from man's inability to sit quietly in a room alone'. That's Blaise Pascal in giving us permission to come apart and rest awhile (if you can!) And that's Jesus, by the way!

Chapter Four:

Rezooming Where We Left Off

Time: the capacity to stand outside yourself, above yourself and move quickly and backwards through a ménage of memory. Time: a stream meandering from the past towards the other country that is the future. Strangely immersed in its secret flow, we are caught, inexorably held in the living current of history for a while; prisoners to a movement that rushes us forward, ever forward. Those who dwelt in the strange land of the past did not realise they were living in history. They were inhabitants of the NOW. For we are, let it be said, an older version of our younger self; unfolding chronology of time and experience cautions us from telling a story from the perspective of journey's end.

Experiences of the past and expectations of the future are knit together into a linear progression. Time moulds the human continuity. It provides inner coherence and identity, enabling yourself to rise above yourself and write a narrative that integrates time past with time present. This mental task we call history, or biography to bring it into the lives of the personal, indeed of four men, moving on in the flow of the years who gathered one end of an April evening. Each was a very different person, as indeed all are strangers to themselves.

The man or woman has yet to live who could fully and sympathetically appreciate the living soul of another, except by the many windows and doors that permit both light and exchange. Our powers and our weaknesses, our development and our constraints; our capacities and deficiencies render us a riddle both unread and unreadable by benign others.

Courtesy of the pandemic network tool of choice, it was Liam who played host on Zoom, sending out the invitations and admitting each in turn.

Liam – Ah, there we all are! There's Bill – welcome, Bill! Welcome, Steve! Great to see you.

Steve – Well, well! After all this time, we meet again. Don't know where Jack has got to.

Bill – Brilliant to see you, Steve! Think we last spoke.... well, how long ago?

Steve – Must be six years. What a lot of life has come and gone. Ah here's Jack. Hi, brother! Turn your microphone on! We can't hear you.

Jack – Evening Steve, evening all! Liam, Bill – it's been a long time. Far too long.

Jack - I know it's only six where you are, but here in India it's half-past one in the morning!

Liam – We won't keep you, but great to catch up. So, how are we all finding this weird time? Don't think our world has ever had such a surprising interruption to all the frenetic activity!

Bill – Affects us all but we all experience it differently. Depends what life was for us BC (before Covid). For me, as a researcher writing astronomy papers, it doesn't feel too different except I can't socialise or go out too much.

Steve – For me, it's extremely taxing. My software business is right on all these ways we are engaging with each other, video-conferencing and all that. But customers are like rain in the Mojave Desert back in California.

Liam – And how's Amanda?

Steve - Mandy is still doing her human rights law work but many Courts and clients have put things on hold. Our son, Ben, though, is in a flat in London and I suspect the situation is taking its toll on his mental health. He's often had his wobbles, as you know. Think he's finding out what profound isolation can feel like, though we try to keep in touch most days.

Jack – We're doing ok too, thanks. Liz had her brush with breast cancer a couple of years back but the charity we're involved with to help the Dalits is strapped for cash. Thousands of untouchables are starving under the lockdown, so it's pretty grim. One positive is that the incessant blaring of horns is much subdued. We still miss our son Timothy every day. Liam?

Liam – Can't get out like anyone else, but like millions, I'm suddenly immersed in this social video eco-system. At first, there was a shared mourning for all we have lost but I guess many of us are finding alternatives. I can look at my diary of speaking engagements and there is, in effect, a line through each of them saying 'cancelled'.

Bill – I'm fortunate to have Katie here with me. Every day I thank God I agreed to bring her up. She has her struggles but doing all right after she broke up with her boyfriend. Trouble is, he sends her revenge porn and it bothers her quite a lot. Her friend, Maddy, is a trainee nurse and is now on the front line. Katie's quite concerned. Maddy is right in the thick of it.

Jack – Tough call! Hope she stays safe! Be great to see her again at some point.

Bill – Thanks. Katie's concerned too about some of the children on the radar of the school. They were struggling learners, many of them. They are having to cope with the intensity of the pressure cooker at home. In one household she knows, the Mum is locked down with a terrorist of an abusive partner. How horrendous is that!

Steve – Ghastly! Hope the police are on it. Must say it's good to have a break from the frenetic pace. After what happened as we were leaving California, I was able to re-assess things, as you know. Now I can notice the flowers and when we go out, we take in the clean air and clear soil. Guess we've all lost our temper at one point or other. We certainly have.

Bill – And we can look up and see stars! Wonderful.

Liam – And we can go out and be thankful that we have another whole day to live! How cool is that! Our obsessive perfectionism, our urge to succeed is all so challenged by this.

And so the old friends talked.

For twenty minutes they talked, a minute for each year. Each marvelled in their own way at the capacity of old friendship to pick up where you left off, to resume from frozen moments.

They began on the edge but then began to move into the centre, remembering that for at least three of the present company, past such moments had led towards a black hole. How close would they now get? There were, Steve had heard, different pandemic personality types. How do we do this when there is no 'how to survive pandemic' guide available? Whether a wise stance was 'Accepting, Suffering or Resisting' occupied five minutes or so.

It seemed that, with one exception, they had all been thrown by the shuttering of their world, not knowing how they were supposed to or work out what they were supposed to do. Bill said he found perspective looking up at stars, peering through an inky night in search of the friendly face he knew was there. This was a cosmic moment, though only a moment.

Steve said he had become an NHS volunteer. It emerged that Mandy was not doing so well really. She was vulnerable and, what with the wheelchair, mobility wasn't straightforward. The feeling of things being out of her control and being unable to escape the situation was imprisoning. There were days at first when she hadn't even wanted to get dressed. It felt like their Dalmatian was sitting on her chest. Rubin just sat there unwilling to move. Their daughter worked in a care home where Covid-19 had slipped through the careful defences.

"It's pretty bad," said Steve. "Last week, Jane thought she had it and had to go back and quarantine. They managed by her isolating in the spare room. Her two-year-old couldn't understand why he wasn't allowed to go in to see Mummy and kept trying the door. The footsteps and plaintiff cries tore Jane in half until the danger passed and life zipped itself".

Her colleague, Ovidio, had been unwell but, as he had mild symptoms and no underlying health conditions, quarantined himself at home. Six days later, he phoned the ambulance. On the seventh day, he messaged his family to say he was deteriorating rapidly. What a difference a week makes. Intensive care; ventilator – it was too no avail. After another week had gone by, Ovidio drew his last gasp. An angel sat and held his hand at the last. "Nothing will replace the physical contact when someone dies," he observed. At that moment, Bill had vivid memories of Katie's Mum, Ali, dying of AIDS in the days of another plague.

Liam agreed. He had taken another funeral that week. Telling people they can't go to a funeral felt pretty harsh. In the strange paradox love takes sometimes, it was a compassionate move. Samsungs came up as the coffin went down. Dozens had Zoomed in, 80% present.

Jack said that India had experienced extended lockdown but few cases so far. Accused of being a virus super-spreader, the previous week, a Muslim guy was dragged away and beaten until blood oozed from his nose and everywhere. So much for Covid being a Muslim plot.

And that was that. A reunion online. Steve's suggestion of "Let's do this again" was well received. Liam said he would send email links for next Thursday. And they left the meeting.

"All well, Dad?" enquired Katie, putting her head round the door. "Dinner's ready."

"Yes, fine," confirmed Bill. "It was good to talk, as they say."

He went into the kitchen.

"This wretched thing was hovering at the edge of consciousness for a while but now the virus hangs like a grey cloud over everything," he remarked. "It's the main topic of talk."

"Sure does," agreed Katie. "Seems to be affecting lower-paid workers and taking a toll especially on ethnic minorities. My friend Maddy says that many of the nurses she knows who have died were Filipino. They came to find a better life and look what happened!"

"Mind you," she added, "some of our school families are having to cope with dwindling resources to put food on the table and pay the rent."

"Structural inequalities, they call it," Bill observed. "Poorer people are dying twice as fast."

They ate in sobering silence.

"Going to chat again?" asked Katie.

"Next Thursday," said Bill, pouring himself a glass. He had enjoyed that encounter. How honest would they be if the road of memory took them through the minefield of the past?

"Including Beth in this conversation?" said Katie suddenly. "It's all men in that Zoom time."

"Hmm", said Bill, gazing intently at her. He wondered what she knew of the disturbing part Steve had played in her life. Beth tried to come over from New York every other Easter.

That had to be called off. It was hard not being with folk you were used to being with.

"See Robert over the road tonight?" Bill asked with a smile, changing the subject.

"Yes, I did," replied Katie. "He was there when we clapped the health workers."

They had exchanged smiles and waves. Tomorrow, they would join a Neighbourhood What's App pub quiz. That morning, there was a note amidst the car wipers. It had a mobile number.

Bill decided to email Beth.

Dear Beth,

I was sad you couldn't come over for Easter as we are used to. It would have been excellent to have seen you. Loneliness is sharper on the days when you are not supposed to be alone. Fortunately (for me), Katie has moved in to hunker down here until her flat sale goes through, whenever that will be! Here, the Government has introduced new housing laws to boost tenants' rights: a ban on no-fault evictions and so on. It'll help a great deal to reduce the uncertainty for those that might miss the rent that month: we'll see how that works out. Katie is getting quite a bit of revenge porn from Freddie, sadly.

I can't get my head round what's happening to our poor world and I don't suppose anyone can. Life is changing so rapidly that this time last week feels like years in the past. 'Life is what happens when you are busy making other plans' – that's Lennon, of course. How far away from where you guys are now was he killed, incidentally? I was reading the other day that his killer, Mark Chapman, confessed in an interview. 'I thought if I killed him, I would become him, I would acquire his fame.' It's interesting, isn't it? The loss of your own value makes you seek the value of someone else. Maybe that's what happens in acts of violence. They create a force-field like those I studied in physics. All kinds of transactions take place. Now there's a thesis for someone!

Speaking of transactions, I was in the local supermarket today. You hand over a note and they look at you and say 'No, no, no, we don't want that –use contactless because it's safer than handling grubby money'. The demise of cash? Discuss!

Expect you are able to work remotely. How's that? Got any work at the moment?

I had a very vivid dream last night. You wandered in and out! We're having to process a huge amount of stress and collective anxiety. Maybe it shows up in dreams. Wonder what the mental health and well-being is like in New York? The fact that lots seem to be having vivid dreams shows our collective psyche is over-charged, I reckon.

What I wanted to mention, though, is that I had a reunion earlier. It was on Zoom but worth doing once you get past the slightly tinny voices. Liam was there and acted as host. You will imagine who else? Steve and Jack: I can't remember if you ever met Jack. In this virus-laden world, I'll guess that in view of what passed between you and Steve twenty years ago, you wouldn't want to meet. That would be laden with another kind of heaviness. So, there we were, friends reunited from the fateful day. Speaking of emotionally charged history, San Francisco will have too many memories for you, I'm sure, but wonder what's going on there. E-mail me if you can about the situation in your part of New York.

For now, I send you my very fondest best wishes,

Bill

Later, after he and Katie had gone to their own rooms, Bill lay there trying to get to sleep. Through the unquiet moments of tossing night, recollections jostled for attention.

Six days had passed since meeting Liam. When next in California, Bill took his new friend from Britain to an Ideas Group he attended just below Telegraph Hill. Bill said that the group convened monthly, rotating its venue round seven or eight regulars. It had started a year ago, the inspiration of Andrew Calvin, a Berkeley physicist. They were drawn together in fascination with a fine-tuned universe that mesmerised all who gazed with wonder.

The door of the apartment was opened by a man in his mid-fifties. His face was long and thin as if his head had been compressed. He looked slightly odd, an impression compounded by an incongruous combination of designer jeans and an old cardigan. But there was natural warmth about Andrew Calvin that quickly made Liam feel at home.

"Come on in. Hi, Bill. And Liam. You're very welcome!" he said with a smile. They walked into the main room. Five men and two women were standing or sitting. One of the women was not joining in other conversations but stood gazing out of the window. This extraordinarily beautiful lady turned and looked directly at him, with hair that seemed to dance like it should in a shampoo advert.

"Beth, meet Liam," said Bill, introducing his guest.

They talked for a few minutes before other hands were shaken. Liam didn't catch all their names. Each was involved in some field of science. After a drink, the routine exchange of news fell silent, comfortable chairs were occupied and preliminaries enacted. As the evening moved on and they exchanged book reviews and comment, Liam was intrigued by their conversation and their openness to a spiritual dimension. He was introduced.

"You must come and talk to us sometime," said Andrew Calvin. "Beth has prepared something for us tonight so we'll now turn to her now, if that's OK."

There are not many jobs for a professional philosopher apart from being a professor. Most of those trained, degreed and gowned in the subject ended up in other walks of life. Like the San Francisco Police Department. Beth was a vehicle examiner who applied logic to working out the causes of accidents. It required careful sifting of the evidence, always searching for causes; immediate causes, first causes and causes of causes.

Beth began to talk, without notes and almost without breath.

"For four centuries," she said, "religion and science held to their exclusive way of looking at the world. Science was for the real world, for medicines, weapons, engineering. Religion was for poetry and wonder, the uncertain, the indefinable. But now science has come round to talking about a moment of creation. Even Einstein had to accept the evidence for an expanding universe and the implication that everything started off one dark night."

Beth paused, her brows knotted as she struggled for expression. "It would be breath-taking if, instead of being an enemy, science was helping to unveil the face of the Creator. But I honestly think that's where we're headed. Some very elegant theories have been built about how something comes from nothing. That time and space switched on spontaneously as if it's all been explained and can we go onto the next problem now?"

"It looks convenient," she went on. "The gap between nothing and something is bridged with a tremor that sparks it all off. Nothing has a hiccough. Next thing you know, something is waving at us. Suddenly, they've pulled 70 billion galaxies out of their hats. But wait a minute! Wait a minute! Either there is nothing to begin with, no time, no quantum vacuum and no physical laws, or there's something. And that something needs explaining!"

Beth went on, with the air of a practised debater you hoped was on your side. "Almost all physicists start their account of how the universe came into being with the laws of nature. But where do the laws that shaped everything come from? We have grown accustomed to its face, but why is there a universe to begin with and why did it form this way?"

Beth said it ran counter to all our human experience to say that we must just accept the existence of things. When we look at the universe, we instinctively ask the question 'how has all this come to be?' Every explanation leaves us with something that is uncaused and not dependent on anything else for its existence".

"Don't you think they've explained how the universe came into existence?" interrupted a man whose name Liam had missed.

"Don't you believe it," said Andrew Calvin dismissively.

Bill nodded his head. "We've learnt to live with the way things are. But it's far, far more likely that there should be nothing rather than something. Either that or there ought to be total chaos. Anything other than this fine-tuned cosmos we see everywhere."

Andrew Calvin nodded. "And of course, no explanation of the universe can be taken seriously unless it can account for some basic observations, some of which are quite recent," he said.

"What do you mean?" asked Liam, looking round at these brilliant people who were yearning to restore wonder to Third-Millennium people.

"I think we're in for a long evening," said Bill.

Within that group, Liam thought, the wonder was definitely growing, the curious mystery of the beginning of time itself, the wonder of a mysterious event that unfolded the entire cosmos. They said that the starting-pistol was a Big Bang. Perhaps it was a flower unfolding with breathtaking speed and the whole structure of everything was profoundly biological.

"It is for us all to interpret this evidence," Beth concluded. "I have come to believe that science and faith are converging. Both need expanding to include a wider picture of the other. From being traditional sparring partners, who knows if their marriage won't be the great social event of the new Millennium?" And after the Q and A, discussion wound up.

"That was very moving!" Bill said as they returned home.

"Tell me more about Beth," Liam asked curiously. "She speaks freely and there's a buzz about her. Her words feed my sense of wonder. But when she talks about herself, her voice and expression drop as if hiding a loneliness her mind doesn't somehow touch."

"Oh, she has mysterious depths all right," said Bill. "She's definitely got star quality."

"Is she married or in a relationship?" Liam wondered.

"To her friends," said Bill, "this is one of the cosmic mysteries. You'd think someone would have grabbed her heart. Recently, she's found this guy. The only snag is, he's married".

"What about her faith then?" wondered Liam.

Bill shook his head. "Beth is, or was, a practising Catholic. But there's a void inside that she's never allowed her faith to connect with. Beth enjoys keeping her distance. If anyone gets too close, they'll reach into her inner being. Now she's met someone who has found a way in."

They drove on in silence. Then Bill added, with a tangible lament in his voice, "Why did it have to be a man she couldn't have? It's like a Greek tragedy playing itself out."

"Who is he?" Liam asked.

"His name is Steve Bright."

Liam looked quizzical, trying to disguise a knotted expression that formed on his forehead. He knew that name.

"I gather that Steve Bright is the owner of a software design company here in Silicon Valley," Bill said. I'm told that Amanda, his wife, has a growing reputation as a human rights lawyer. I knew Steve Bright at school once. I met his brother a couple of years ago on a cruise liner."

A week later, they had gone for dinner with Beth. She lived alone in a sizeable house that once belonged to her father. He had moved to Marin County when he began to do well financially, in the days when it was full of cocaine enthusiasts. Bill went to talk to Beth about his Ali. Liam glanced through a paper, sticky with a new age feel. Therapists and practitioners offered rebirthing and astral travel.

"How come you work for the famous SFPD?" Liam asked, as drinks entered, courtesy of this elegant woman with long black hair.

Beth smiled and her curls seemed to dance in symbiotic waltz.

"While I was doing my degree," she said, "Watergate broke. Raised in the liberal era of the 60s, this was the final stage of disillusionment just at the time I was forming opinions about everything."

She paused to pour herself a drink.

"It made me cynical about leadership and institutions. I saw that truth and justice have to be fought for. We're always only one step away from corruption. Rather than stay in academia, I looked round for a job where I can make a difference. Idealistic, but there it is," she added.

"Any regrets?" Liam was curious.

"Not really. When I hear philosophers talk these days, I'm not sorry I left the intellectual establishment. Three years ago, I went to the 19th World Congress of Philosophy at Boston. Philosophy is so tribal, so balkanised. All those Aristotelians and Nietzscheans, Marxists and logicians, neo Kantians and ethics experts; all jostling together, talking to their own tribe. Like Babel, a dialogue of the deaf!"

"Philosophy can be very stimulating but it can also be as empty as the void within the human soul," observed Liam.

Beth smiled faintly. "I studied Heidegger, once acclaimed round the world but whose life played out the spiritual tragedy of our times. In 1945, as his beloved Nazis were at their last gasp, the most elevated statement that formed on his lips was 'Being is the trembling of Godding'. It was all hot air; chasing after wind, as the old book of Ecclesiastes puts it."

"How come you know Bill?" asked Liam.

Beth told him that she met Bill after his wife had died in a car accident. She had been one of the investigators working out the cause. A friendship developed.

"Strictly platonic, right, Bill?" she said with a smile.

"Chance would be a fine thing," replied Bill, twinkling.

"And how long have you been a part of that Ideas Group?" Liam was intrigued.

Bill became her spokesman. "After I rebuilt my life, I was looking for something. I introduced Beth to a number of friends. We were all converging in our ideas."

"That's about it," said Beth. "When I investigate an accident, I ask who or what caused it and how did it happen?" She paused to suck the juice out of an orange. "It's daft to say that we mustn't enquire about the existence of things and just accept them", she went on. "All our human experience is against it. When we look at the universe, it's natural to ask the question - how has all this come to be?"

"Only today," she exclaimed, "we were examining an accident the other side of Richmond Bridge. The cause of death seemed to be the driver's airbag that exploded into her face at 150 miles an hour, throwing her against the headrest. "The universe definitely needs explaining. Why is there something rather than nothing? Blind chance? or cosmic accident?"

"Could the universe have given itself birth?" Beth pondered. "We only consider the idea of a universe continually pulsating with life, expanding and contracting, having a Creator, because we are reluctant to face the truth. It is a flight from the light."

And with that, the light increased. Bill realised the day was dawning. It was time to awake.

Chapter Five:

Let's Get Creative

We're used to the idea that Monday to Friday, our time is not our own, but then suddenly it's Friday evening, and there's nothing to do and nowhere to go. Bill was, therefore, glad of Katie's company. She showed him her mobile phone.

"Look at this Dad," she said. "You might be interested to see this email from Maddy."   "Ok, thanks," Bill replied. "Let me have a Zoom time with my old friends and I'll read it. In the meantime, pour yourself this welcome home cuppa."

 Zoom had gone from Conferencing App to Pandemic Social Network. And here they were....

Liam – Evening, everyone! Good to see you again! I'll just admit Jack in India.

Steve – I can see him but there's no sound. Ah, there you are. Hi, Jack.

Jack – Hi, bruv!

Bill – Evening, Jack, what's going on where you are this week?

Jack – Well, as you know, the Modhi announced that the whole country would go into lockdown in four hours' time. That announcement caused panic and utter chaos as millions of daily-paid workers and others left megacities like Mumbai to try and get back to their families in the rural areas. As trains and buses stopped, many were left to find their way home on foot. Now, millions of families are locked down in cramped conditions. Often as many as six people in one room. They are not allowed to work. It's pretty stark.

Bill – Sounds like it. Is there nothing to cheer us up this evening?

Steve – Well, anyone getting creative? Mandy thinks the garden has never looked so good!

Liam – So, if we're having a bad news moratorium, I can announce I am halfway through the French cookbook. Lots of new recipes I will insist on trying you on when we meet again.

Bill - In his great book about the positives of ageing, Cicero said we should learn something new every day. The illiterate of the 21st century will not be those who cannot read and write, but those who cannot learn, unlearn, and relearn. Or so I keep telling myself....

Jack – Liz and I have been trying to paint. Haven't done any since we saw those pictures Timothy did in his bedroom. To this day, can't even draw the curtains. But Liz persuaded me.

Bill- I've been having a go at a story.

Liam, Jack, Steve –Well, share it! What's it about?

Bill – ....

Liam – You muted suddenly? I think you're saying something profound but get off 'mute'!

Bill – I was saying we won't be returning to the old world we left two months ago so why not try new tricks?

Liam – Guys, I've got an idea. The number one topic of whoever we're with is the virus, right? So why don't we get creative as a reunion group and do some creative writing?

Steve – Good idea! What story could we tell?

Jack – Most painters have stressed the emotional importance of art. Art helps us through. Same principle, I imagine. It keeps us connected to the radiant feeling of being alive. Not that you'd know it from my watercolours!

Bill – We all need something that enables us to keep going, that takes us out of ourselves.

Liam – The greats in their field have done what they've done because they did it with great intensity. The excitement and exhilaration, and all that.

Steve – That's what they call 'flow'. I got to some of that with the start-up in California.

Jack – I've got to go in a mo, but let's get creative in this way then. Try it.

Steve – Guess it needn't be about our own life-story. It'll be an interesting change from gardening. Might involve Mandy, who sends her love, by the way.

Bill – Could be about anybody.

Liam – I must go too, but may I suggest we start scribbling and compare notes in a week or two? By the way, Bill, from how you look now, think yours is going to be a shaggy dog story!

Steve recollected one such reunion about ten years ago – he couldn't pin down exactly. The old friends had met in a country club hotel; a pressure-free zone, a four-star hideaway that offered country pursuits for the initiated or complete indulgence to relieve the aching mind and tone up those muscles. From its terrace, an October evening sun daubed an entire landscape with a glow that was almost eerie. At times orange, at times green, the light had gently sought out the true nature of things, lending every image sharper focus.

On the green opposite, several people had walked their dogs, enjoying the enthusiasm with which they ran to fetch the sticks that were being thrown in teasing, repetitive action. A pair of bull terriers were in a state of over-excitement, their high spirits making them belt round the green. Like lovers, they could not bear to be parted. One of them howled like a mad thing when the owner got hold of its friend and insisted it was time to go.

They would meet again. 'We'll meet again'. And with that, they signed off. It was so decided. Each would now ponder what they could bring to the party and get scribbling.

Bill read the email from Katie's friend, Maddy; sombre yet hopeful, in a chatty sort of way.

Hi, Katie,

This is tough; the toughest time I can remember. It's a psychological and economic pandemic as well as a public health emergency. People are being hit differently. We're not in the same boat, but we are most definitely in the same storm. For my mates in the States, this is their 9/11 moment. We'll all talk about this when we're old; what it was like to live through a profound trauma shared by everyone else. So, I've decided to join up, you might say, just like my Great-Granddad did in the war. Nurse training can continue afterwards but right now I'm working in a paramedic team on the front-line but absolutely no hero.

I'll send you a pic. My day starts at 4 in the morning and the shift doesn't end until 6 at night. Our unit is the first medical team seen by patients and possibly the last their families will see. I had to tell someone today they couldn't ride in the ambulance so that was a permanent goodbye. It has me in tears most days but I wouldn't swap it with anyone.

For my younger sister, Maryanne, whom you remember, it's not exactly easy either, what with her A-levels being cancelled this year. It's like she was preparing to run the marathon and had come to the start line. They were counting down, 3, 2, 1 - and suddenly they tell you they're not going to run the race. Feels like she can't close her school chapter properly but can't distract herself by going out. Should she spend her days doing revision or what? I think the loss of routine and uncertainty around grading have affected her. What she used to do to manage her anxiety following a strict routine that got her out of the house is not an option at the moment. This is having a big effect on anyone like Maryanne with an existing mental health condition. She's lost her coping mechanisms, contact with friends or routines that helped. But then, anyone who was doing their coursework or end of year assignments is in the same boat. All those rites of passage graduations and proms – such a shame!

I guess handling loss of routine is facing most of us. For me, it's not been hard to find new routines. Obviously, I'm not allowed to see my boyfriend John. Sex aside, kissing's a riskier act in a pandemic where you have to have face masks! John had been working in a bar but that's now been shut down. Heard from Freddie?

Talk soon. Maddy.

"Wow", exclaimed Bill. "Thanks for sharing that!" "What a courageous young lady."

"Pretty awesome," agreed Katie. She cocked her head in Bill's direction as she stirred something in a pot. "Dad, you're getting really quite hairy you know?!"

"I know," said Bill. "Feel I'm quite oh so Michael Jackson! The guys just joshed about that."

"Maybe I should fix you up with the League of Underground Hairdressers," joked Katie. "I hear they'll be in the area next Thursday!" They both laughed. Bill looked at Katie lovingly.

He remembered when she had first met Freddie. Among hordes of guys in jeans and trainers standing at the bar, one had stood out. "See that chap?" Katie indicated with a quiet jab of the finger. Bill raised his eyebrows. And that's where it started. Freddie was definitely in the past tense. Katie lived with Freddie for some time; no doubt attracted to the suave successful image he projected. But it all turned to dust. Freddie was a control freak. He just had to be the centre of attention. He checked her texts. If Katie phoned any of her friends, he made a fuss, stomping around making sarcastic comments. But when the call was over, Freddie would go back to ignoring her. He didn't want her to have any happiness outside their relationship. Everything had to be done his way or not at all. His unforgiving nature and his moods spoilt the relationship. Eventually, Katie couldn't stand it. They sold the flat.

That wasn't the end of it. Freddie pursued her strongly, now with revenge porn. He became dictatorial and unpredictable. Last year, he crashed his car being way over the limit and was banned for a year. His company was taking disciplinary action. It was not good for the image.

Ever since she was 18, Katie had had a series of unrewarding relationships, mostly with black guys. Lasting love had always eluded her. When she was at college, she pursued a likely lad with a gusto that surprised the most hardened men. Freddie was one of her conquests but then the boot was on the other foot. Bill thought this dispassionately, as if describing someone else. But inside, he felt a great weight of sadness, his balding head glistening with little beads of sweat.

"Seen any more of that chap over the road?" Bill probed. "You seem to have been doing a lot of texting every time we sit down to absorb ourselves in Netflix. Must be more compelling!"

"Definitely, detective Dad!" and they both laughed.

"We've got a lot in common. Robert is not in a relationship before you ask! He's harmless!"

"I guess what we're pining for is something that goes to the core of our being. Love is all you need," Bill said. Not for the first time, he wondered if we were not the Elastoplast generations, who had left a little bit of stick with each of their partners until there was no more stick left. We never did get to the freedom of the Promised Land.

And he thought of Beth in New York. And Sarah, his long-since past wife.

The unending cosmos inside the soul of an astronomer still haunted him. A moving escalator conveyed Bill to a degree in astronomy from the University of Washington and a PhD at the University of California. There was still a reverberation of those heady days of the 60s. The Free Speech movement and opposition to the war in Vietnam were embedded in the sacred tradition. By the early 70s, the world was no longer poised for change. After various posts in NASA came and went, it was to recapture something that he returned to San Francisco to lecture at Berkeley; a man who loved his job and who loved his wife. In that order.

Marriage to Sarah didn't go well. His Dad disliked her from the start as if protective of what Mum might have said. Perhaps he could sense she would be difficult to handle. By degrees, acid was poured over their relationship. Love was corroded away. Bill's emotions wandered.

Other women caught his eye. Sarah was distraught and could no longer control herself. Gradually, she slipped into a drink-fuelled life and sad relationships with other men. One day, he walked out. He needed time. Bill went on a long cruise to think things over. It was there he heard Sarah had died in a freeway pile-up. Bill blamed himself for her death. The destruction of a human being lay heavy upon him. One day, she would come walking back through that door and relieve him of the burden. For two years, he had been a lost soul.

People had not known what to say to him when Sarah died. Politics, religion and sex were now acceptable topics of conversation, but death was not. He found he could talk to Beth who had descended into death and was finding hope. Beth was a lot more connected inside generally, though it pained Bill that there was an emotional blockage of some sort when it came to holding baby Katie or playing with her. She seemed a little cold to the child, as though not fully accepting of her. Bill put it down to her being unsure how to relate to youngsters since losing her own baby. What a cosmos we have inside us.

Bill wandered outside. He gazed at a night sky and stars that tip-toed through the chimneys.

The Universe. Its boundaries are uncertain; its limits limitless. If there is an end, what would lie beyond that end? If one could sail to the furthest boundary of everything, what lies over the horizon? Have we reached the edge?

Some say that the universe is a giant sphere and to arrive is to have returned to the place from where the journey began. Others contend the universe is a hall of mirrors where the light is bent round, and what we behold is a reflection of other galaxies in the silent expanse in which we dwell. Or that we are unknowing inhabitants of one universe amongst many.

In a voyage of the imagination, leave behind mysteries that dwell in the outer limits of everything. Go quickly past expanding galaxies and shrinking stars, past galaxies that are vast spiral nebulae and galaxies like catherine wheels in a firework display. Leave Galactic superclusters behind like lights along a motorway; each galaxy a metropolitan community of stars with many times more inhabitants than the largest cities on planet Earth. Flash past ten hundred thousand million suns spread out over oceans of empty space. Past beautiful Andromeda, the galaxy next door. Now we have arrived at the Milky Way. Star upon star rushes by. There is a spiral arm. Imperceptibly, we are being dragged round the heart of the galaxy on a journey that takes 250 million years. All human history could be comprehended within a tiny fraction of one turn on that stately circuit.

And here is a medium-size yellow star with a small family of orbiting planets; balls of gas or rock spending a million lifetimes in a frenzied dash around it. The third globe is a blue and white island. Descending through layers of a thin air-cushion, the imagination glides gently down. On one continent, a range of hills stands to attention above a throbbing city. As the Earth spins, day is now night. It is a clear, crisp night. On the hillside stands a tree. In the tree there sits a man. He peers, gazes, slowly mesmerised by the heavens as he imagines a journey such as this through clouds of memory and dancing stars.

Was there any purpose, any cosmic plan in a world where people's lives were split and split again? Though he often lectured about the stars, Bill wished he could be sitting up the tree once more, hearing the stars whisper friendly talk to his face.

That was then. This is now. Bill poured himself a drink. But here was a note from lovely Beth.

Chapter Six:

In the Days of the Plague

How great to hear from Beth! If Bill's other partners in crime were going to tell a story, Beth needed to tell hers, though not for the consumption of anyone else. This was private.

Dear Bill,

Fantastic to hear from you! It was good to hear that Katie's doing well. It would be really good to hear that she can find the pathways of true love and not go in for someone who won't cherish her as she deserves.

Sounds like your commitment to bringing her up has paid off richly these past twenty years. I very much wish now I could have been a Mum substitute to this beautiful black girl who lit up our lives.

You asked if I'm working remotely and the answer is yes. I feel guilty that knowledge-workers like me are in a privileged position. To have to expose yourself to this thing out of financial necessity is dire; even more so if you might risk contaminating someone in a care facility. My cleaner is not, of course, coming to support me during the crisis – no real need. But her other job is working in a home that looks after dementia people. So easily she could take it with her and this deadly enemy has found a cunning way through the defences. But what can she do? She needs to work in order to put food on the plate for her two-year-old.

The pandemic is sharpening racial divides in society. Because medical care and drugs here are in the hands of those who are driving for profit the whole time, there's little sense of public good in capitalism. Being predatory doesn't make you a capitalist. It makes you a sociopath! Drugs are 50% more expensive over here. Health care is calculated as if you are a profit-centre. More and more, I'm questioning the whole system. You guys are so fortunate!

So, here I am in the most intense place in the country. It's all concentrated in one little slice of land. New York is a city of carnage, or to change the picture, a ghost town. Those who can have left. People got fired rather than being laid off for a while. Covid is a profound attack on our way of life. The news is very troubling and confusing. Should we go out or should we stay in? We don't have control over Covid. But what we can control is our behaviour. Faith really helps. Without it, the world is a puzzle, death is a horror movie and eternity a blank.

All this got out of control very quickly because people didn't take it seriously or because they blamed everyone else. Democracies are not spectator sports. We have to know what's going on so we go along with it. For a long time, we've seen rising levels of political polarisation in the USA due to mutual hatred and incomprehension. We have been on a downward path. Who will bring us out? It will take better leadership than this.

You and I were both in San Francisco in the days of another plague. You remember how the gay community felt stigmatised at first and closed ranks. Then they let experts in – hooray!

Those years working in that Aids unit are a time to be treasured. I never regretted swapping being a vehicle examiner for that. Vivid memories of Ali's last days are sharper recently.

Thanks for telling me about Steve. All that is firmly in the past but I don't believe I would like to Zoom in with him.

Bill, you're a good man and amongst my regrets are that we never crossed the emotional threshold – let alone any other kind! Maybe in one of your parallel universes, we are together. So, let's stay close and give an ample sufficiency of hugs (in sort of a nod to Jane Austen whom I am reading right now).

Warm wishes,

Beth

―――――――――――――――――

Well, that chewed Bill up for the rest of the evening. Beth had given him constant updates about Ali when she was dying of AIDS.

One day, twenty years before, Liam had come for one of his periodic speaking visits. They sipped a take- away coffee in Golden Gate Park.

"Look at that!" said Beth in sudden awe, glancing at a flower that had spread its leaves towards them for inspection. They watched, fascinated, as a butterfly emerged from a chrysalis. In every life, Liam remarked, there are seasons of anguish and desperation that can mean the end or can equally bring a turning point. Beth said how often she had longed for her inner being to be reborn and break free from anchors that moored her to the past.

At that moment, a lady walked by. Beth recognised her.

"Hello, Su Lin," she said with pleasure, jumping up to greet her friend. They engaged in small talk for a few minutes. Liam wondered if he should leave them to it.

"Su Lin once shared a house with me," said Beth, introducing her friends to each other. "Su-Lin was really into scientology then," she remarked.

Su Lin said she was wanting a spiritual side in her life when she met a group of people who seemed to have answers.

"I see through it now but if you saw a group of people who lived in community and who were interested in no war, no crime, who said we've got to look after the planet and respect other people, many people would be drawn."

"Yes...." agreed Liam, "our search for those things is beautiful and good, though we look in the wrong places, I believe."

"You're right. Look, I must go," said Su Lin and they said goodbye. As she was walking off, she paused before turning back.

"I must tell you," she said to Beth. "Yesterday in the AIDS unit where I work, I met someone who knows you. I can't remember how we made the connection."

"What's her name?" asked Beth.

"Ali, I think."

"Sure," said Beth, alert with interest. "Bill's friend is somewhere in San Francisco but all he knows is that she has AIDS. Is it very advanced?"

"It's getting that way."

"How long has she got?"

"Three months. Maybe more. Maybe less."

Three months! Su Lin hesitated. "Look, I have to be ultra-careful about patient confidentiality," she said. "I can't reveal appointment times. But it breaks my heart to think of anyone facing death alone. If you come tomorrow at four, you might just bump into Ali."

At four the next day, Beth went to the AIDS clinic. It depressed anyone who remembered San Francisco as a sunny place to be and the centre of the hippy movement. Afterwards, amidst an indifferent atmosphere, the gay community had grown rapidly. Then the plague had struck. Behind the postcards, it was no longer a summer of love but a city of grief.

Su Lin had just watched someone die.

"It's too awful," she said.

"Thanks," she managed a smile, taking a report from a young man, obviously an official person of some sort but who didn't seem like a doctor.

"Is he a nurse?" Beth asked.

"No, he's a volunteer. You become part of an AIDS ward team or volunteer programme because your lover is infected. These people know they might be next. Many gay men around here have buried twenty of their friends."

"Sometimes I reach the point where I just can't go on. You're personally involved. We've all nursed friends. With every patient, you relive the tragedy."

"Our generation had those searing experiences of war in Vietnam," observed Beth. "But I've heard that more people have died of AIDS in the US than in the entire war out there."

"What about the risk to Ali's child, though?" Beth asked. "Will she die?"

"I can give you the stats," said Su Lin. "Three-quarters of children with AIDS are still alive after their fifth birthday. But it's by no means certain that Ali's little girl will be infected by HIV or go on to develop full-blown AIDS. I'm not sure who is looking after her right now."

"What about this new miracle drug, AZT?" Beth asked.

"There's still no cure though AZT does slow down the virus in some cases."

"But what happens now to Ali? What's she to expect?"

Su Lin paused. How much should she tell?

"Ali is already experiencing constant diarrhoea, weight loss and tiredness. And she's often getting unwell, fighting for breath. That means she has a chest infection. But the symptom we have to watch most is deterioration of the brain. Once AIDS attacks the brain, people experience difficulties in thinking, coordination and memory."

Beth had never realised before how much impotence felt like fear.

But there, in front of them, was a young lady who could only be Ali.

"Hello, Ali," said Beth. "Remember me?"

"You look familiar. Beth? Beth! I'm so glad to see you," said a frightened hesitant voice as recognition lit up a worn, haggard face. It was a far cry from a confident bright and breezy person Beth knew slightly though mostly mediated through what Bill told her.

They sat talking for 20 minutes. "Meet Bill," Beth pleaded. "He's desperate to see you."

"I would like to see him," said Ali. "I don't want to die all by myself. Where is he?"

"At this moment, Bill's in Germany. He gets back in early October, though I expect he will want to fly back immediately once he has heard from you."

"No," said Ali. "Please. Don't interrupt his work. Tell him I insist he wait until the job is finished. I'll still be here...I'm not going anywhere."

"What's happened to..?"

"Linda? Oh, she left a year ago. The strain on the relationship broke it in two. I guess she feels responsible for what happened, as it was her brother who gave this to me."

"And your little girl?"

"Katie's three now and in care. I can't look after her like this."

Beth was overwhelmed with grief. She felt she could easily give up her job and work on an AIDS project, doing something useful with her life. As the century's last autumn wore on, she chatted about this with Su Lin.

"You could enquire at the Shanti project here in San Francisco. The feeling of togetherness is very strong there."

Beth had a strong urge to follow that up. The gift of security and self-acceptance that she was struggling to find in her own life could be used to help people like Ali. Maybe she could turn her wounds into gold.

In late September, Bill returned. Beth had kept in touch with him and told him about Ali. Faithfully and insistently, she passed on Ali's insistence that he not break off his work to fly home until he had finished his assignment.

But, one week, there was a scare. Ali was rushed into hospital. Beth took it on herself to email Bill. He was on the next plane home. Bill was profoundly shocked when he walked into the hospital ward. Memories were immediately recalled from semi-retirement, vivid pictures of visiting his mother when she laying dying. But this was no cancer ward where people were middle-aged or retired. Here was a ward of young people who, until recently, had three-quarters of their lives ahead of them. Ali was sweaty, lying panting on her hospital bed. Wires and tubing invaded the upper part of her body. They were giving her medication to relieve the breathlessness from the pneumonia that stalked AIDS victims.

"Ali!" said Bill. Her hands gripped her father with fear, groping for reassurance. Beneath an oxygen mask, her face managed a thin smile.

"Hi!" she said gladly and held his hand tightly.

They took the mask off for a while so Bill and Ali could talk. Beth left them to it. She wandered around the ward looking at fading lives against a backcloth of some fading roses. What was it like, she pondered, to die like this, deeply scared, in pain and so alone?

"Whatever happens," said Bill. "I'm here for you."

"There is something."

"Tell me," said Bill, trying unsuccessfully to hide his anguish as he held her hand.

"It's Katie," said Ali. "I really want you to look after her if anything happens to me."

"We're a long way from that yet, Ali."

The nurse had told him that Ali would probably get over this illness but not necessarily the next. She gave Ali about two months but that was just a guess.

"I want peace of mind for the future. You know, Beth's been a tower of strength," Ali managed to say in one breath.

"In this latest crisis, she's been bedding down here every night, clinging on to me while I ride the rollercoaster."

They talked for a while. The nurse came to put the mask back on. Bill and Ali said goodbye.

That night Beth sat at her dressing table, slowly combing her black hair. Who or what had given her a heart as wide as the Pacific Ocean she often sat beside as a girl, in the house that once belonged to her father? Explaining the universe was one thing. But despite her own disintegration after the miscarriage, was she any nearer comprehending the unfathomable inside, the inner world of her that begged for explanation? Having given everything, when the black hole threatened she felt she would be suspended over the very nothingness from which the original world had sprung, that her being would dissolve into the chaos from which creation was being continually defended.

It would take much time for Beth to speak freely about the suppressed turmoil that had driven her to clothe herself with protective dignity and keep up a mysterious air. Back then, her hair was still bereft of the curls that made her face so distinctive, though they were beginning to return as the life slowly awoke.

By mid-December, Ali was still in the land of the living. Bill forced himself to view every hour she was alive as a bonus. Deep down, Ali was praying and willing herself to stay with them for a little longer. They laughed and joked and laughed and cried. It was like old times again. But then, he would look at her in her wheelchair, incontinent, thin and with a damaged brain that was impairing her ability to think. That night, Ali died peacefully. Bill sat with her, anguished, yet unaccountably serene. The doctor put the time of death at 4.30 am.

A week later, he and Beth were standing in a Crematorium. No one else showed up. After the service, they stood in the crematorium where Bill had stood all those years ago with a mother-shaped vacuum inside him. Beth was with him, holding Katie, who kept looking around as if expecting Ali to pop around the corner. Eyebrows raised in pain, Bill sniffed into his handkerchief. His soul cried out to God. Another wave rolled in, a crest of sadness. But even in its tumult, Bill felt a peace inside and knew he was acquitted of all charges and words that had ever been levelled against him, even framed by him.

Alone in her room that night, Beth cried once more for Ali, but then Katie cried too and she ran to her as if to blot out the night and make the sun shine again. As she held the little lady tight, it dawned on her that though she was mourning her child who had miscarried, she was accepting the child inside herself. For a moment, the floor fell but then she righted herself and it stopped. It was a moment of integration as when two railway carriages are coupled. Katie slept against her until early morning when Bill came padding in, eyes widening with surprise and pleasure as he saw her there. Beth looked up and whispered her freedom.

"I have accepted the child. I am now one person."

"I don't understand," said Bill.

"It's OK," Beth said softly. "My mind is free of those images. I'm clear. Someday", she added, 'I'll send you the fragments of poetry I wrote when an awful realisation came to me and unwelcome movies began to play. Give that one a few years though," she added quickly.

Remembering all these things, Bill's mind went back to his conversation with his old friends earlier that evening. "There will be no disappearing down a black hole!" he said out loud.

"Pardon?" asked Katie, popping her head round the door.

Bill told her of the Zoom chat and the resolve to be creative. Each of them was to supply a story. He wouldn't get autobiographical but he was so glad that Katie had been in his life!

Chapter Seven:

A Mysterious Disappearance (Bill's Story)

What was he to do on another lockdown day?

After the initial period of wondering how on earth we were all going to get through being confined to our homes, Bill could feel himself changing by the week. It wasn't the superficial response of a New Year's resolve but something far more embedded, richer. There was, coming upon Bill, a growing mood to emulate one of the literary figures he found intriguing and go to the woods to suck the marrow out of life. Except, unlike the poet Henry Thoreau, there were no woods that were accessible. All the pathways to the noticing and the sucking that the woods might offer were denied until further notice. The gates were shut. Yet maybe the closed-in world was calling to him anyway with new horizons. He must live a life he imagined elsewhere.

Across half the world, things were wrapped with an eerie, post-apocalyptic silence. Bill knew that the cities were different. Despite police vigilance, they had never really gone to sleep. Traffic was building up, though, and he knew from friends and media that half of the old life was slowly waking and stretching itself in astonishment. The other half would have to wait for a bit. Little by little, lockdown was being eased. Having required people to stay indoors to protect themselves and everyone else, it was a complicated message to sell that the reverse could now happen, except in fits and starts and hedged with conditions featuring new vocabularies. Everyone was talking about R just as they referred casually to Zoom as if part of their furniture.

R? He had never reproduced personally but becoming Dad to a bewildered little girl had been the single greatest joy in life. Speaking of which, he heard loud laughter.

"What's amusing you, then?" he asked Katie who had just come in.

"Having a laugh with Robert," replied Katie. "We were just trying to do that Italian balcony-singing thing from the other side of the road!

Nessun Dorma will never be the same again but we're not giving up the day job!"

"Think it could go somewhere?" Bill is curious but cautious.

"Wouldn't surprise me," said Katie. "We talk most days now and have lots in common. Can you open yourself, though, after bad experiences? That's the task. But then, you must have found that hard after your wife died in that pile-up and then finding romance blossoming again with my mother, only to find she was a lesbian!"

"It wasn't easy to navigate all that," agreed Bill. "Love to have had something with Beth but she was inaccessible. Like these woods, I just couldn't find a way in."

"But look," he added a little too quickly, "my old partners in crime are working hard at something creative. Not balcony-singing but something written down to share."

"What you going to do?" asked Katie, who had noticed the gear change.

"Befuddled and bemused," said Bill. "Drawn a blank, to be honest."

"I have a suggestion, Dad," Katie said after a pregnant pause. "In that chest upstairs with those old letters and keepsakes, I came across something stapled together you had clearly written once. Why not reprise that?"

"Guess I could dust that down," agreed Bill.

"What's it about?" asked Katie, curiously. "I didn't read too much of it."

Bill drew breath. "You sitting comfortably?" he asked whimsically, and then began.

"The story opens with the disappearance of Joseph Laver, a Professor of Philosophy at Bristol University. His house has been ransacked. He is probably the most famous atheist in the world, regularly wheeled out in chat shows, panel discussions etc., to pour scorn on the existence of God. He has been feted in particular by the North Korean Stalinist regime, desperate to shore up its system in the face of global politics and show that the West is not universally hostile, that here is a famous intellectual who agrees with its stance on the materialist atheism supporting its communism.

"Laver's son, Richard, is called to their father's house by his sister, Jackie. She is very concerned that there is no sign of their dad. When Richard arrives, he is told that word is getting around that recently, Joseph Laver has reversed his whole position. He found dramatic new proof of the existence of God that has caused him to retract.

"Where is he? Who are the people listening in to events in the Professor's house as they unfold? Quickly, those searching the house find a corpse. It is the body of John Lang, Senior Lecturer at the University, sent by Laver to fetch something urgently.

"As the story unfolds, it is clear that Laver is now a prime suspect. He has gone to ground; in fact, he has travelled to Peru, to Macchu Picchu, to provide background material for the Press Conference he will make in a few weeks' time. Both the religious extremist group and the North Koreans listening in to events, have their own reasons for wanting to silence Laver before he goes public with his evidence."

"Ok, so why Macchu Picchu?" Katie asked. "Don't know if we'll ever get there now!"

"It was built by an Inca Emperor who came to the conclusion that there was one God greater than the sun, the focus of Inca worship, so it provides a backdrop," Bill replied.

"En route, the Professor's own thoughts are exposed as to why he has changed his mind and what has led him to see new evidence for the existence of God. Everyone wonders what the Professor has found."

"And that's as far as I got," said Bill rather sheepishly.

"Never mind that!" said Katie with gentle indignation. "Can still be your contribution. Let's work on it together from those notes you made and what you just told me."

The Professor who disappeared

John Lang sat in his car, listening to the storm, watching mighty forces locked in mortal combat around him; raw power; concentrated furious fighting going on in the atmosphere. Lightning forked in massive surges of electricity, a display of raw power combined with a vibrating, jagged voice. Rain threw itself at anyone foolhardy enough to venture out. Thunder shook the house that was his destination. The house was similar to all the others. Tonight, however, floodlit by occasional lightning, the house was the stuff of nightmares.

Many dreams had come and gone. Like Trish. Marriage to a vivacious lady, whose vitality took his breath away, had been good while it lasted. Sadly, Trish was now out of his life. Trish was capable but she was not a warm person. Her mother was not a warm person. Her mother's mother had not been a warm person. Julie was different.

As soon as the worst of the storm abated, John Lang lit a cigarette and walked up the garden path. There was no reason why he should notice the van across the street.

The Professor's instructions were quite clear. No big problem in locating what was needed and bringing it to him. The Professor had explained the situation and John Lang, knowing the increasing tension in recent weeks, was happy to help out.

John Lang wandered around looking for what he had come for. Then he heard sounds from upstairs. He climbed the steps cautiously. He heard his own heart revving up as if on a race track, watching as two men appeared from nowhere. Their presence in the doorway filtered through to him in the same moment as a single shot ran out. His last impulse was a crazy reach for his mobile phone to let Julie know he wasn't going to be able to see her later. Then there was a single explosion in his chest as if he was struck by the lightning he had witnessed earlier. Then there was nothing.

It was the kind of April day that made you feel glad summer was just around the corner.

Not that Richard Laver was in any mood to drink it in. Tiredness had been stalking him since Winchester, a ghost that leered at him down the many miles of the A303 as he pushed on. Not far to go now. He knew he should not be driving. To keep himself awake as his eyelids insisted on doing their own thing, Richard reached for the water bottle on the passenger seat. He opened it and poured some down his neck. The reaction was sharp enough to jerk him back to full consciousness. Not far to go now.

It had been a long twenty-four hours. The flight back from South Africa had been dreary and uneventful and after three weeks out there on a job with the Investment Bank he worked for in London, he was decidedly glad to get back. If it was not for the snoring man occupying the Business Class seat next to him, he might even have caught a few hours rest. Then had come the bus from Heathrow to the train station and an hour later, Richard was sinking into his own bed in Crawley.

The Peugeot purred on across the Wiltshire countryside, eating up the miles. It began to rain, a soft gentle rain that made no demands on anyone. Richard thought of that phone call from his sister Jackie that was as mysterious as it was insistent.

"Richard, its Jackie. Look, I'm really sorry to disturb you and Susan tells me you have only just got back from a business trip."

"Can this wait, Jackie?" he had responded sleepily but puzzled.

"Can you come down to Wells?" she said.

"When?" he asked, with growing puzzlement, sensing that something was very wrong.

"Can you come now, please, Richard? I've had a phone call from a very worried neighbour."

She wouldn't explain over the phone but five words were enough to jerk him out of bed, explain to Susan he needed to go again and to ease his car out of the driveway.

"It's Dad," said Jackie simply. "He has vanished. Not sure if he's been murdered or gone off on the trip he had been talking about."

"I'll be with you in a few hours," he said without hesitation.

Not far now. "Bridgwater 12 miles" proclaimed the sign after turning off the A303 and going what he called 'the back way in' towards the village where Dad lived.

He knew something must have happened that warranted this level of urgency. Jackie had simply said he was not dead, or so she assumed. So where was he?

From far off, Susan had told him about the controversy that was engulfing her father-in-law. It was that report in the Daily Mail that set the cat amongst the pigeons. It was Joseph Laver's fault, she said, and Richard knew what she meant. His father always had a sense of the theatrical. As a boy, stories of how his dad had been the first to climb Everest and had got to the moon before Neil Armstrong had regaled him. Not that his Dad needed building up in his eyes. A Professor of Philosophy at Bristol University had some status attached to it, though not the sort of status that a lively boy could fathom until he was twelve years old. His friends at school, and sometimes his teachers, would bring him newspapers where his father had featured. Or they told him they had seen his dad on the TV. Being the son of probably the most celebrated atheist in the world had some kudos, though it was not the kind of celebrity status that attached itself to the footballer heroes that populated his horizons at that stage.

"You won't believe this!" proclaimed the headline, Susan had said over the phone. It seemed that the most celebrated atheist in the world was reported as deciding after all that he had been wrong all these years. There was much at stake here, Richard observed.

The car settled on the road outside Joseph Laver's home, a familiar sight to Richard and usually a welcome one. His father was not the easiest person to relate to, especially after Mum had died from cancer. Jackie was there to greet him. They hugged.

"What's happened?" Richard asked as they trudged up the drive past Jackie's car and his Dad's Focus Estate.

"See for yourself," she said and opened the door.

Richard could immediately see there was something very out of place from the chaos that greeted him as they stepped over the threshold. Dad was a tidy animal, everything in its place. But not now. The sideboard in the hall had drawers flung open, suspended as if frozen in time. Papers were strewn over the floor.

"If you think this is bad," Jackie said, "look at the study."

Richard obediently followed his sister to the intellectual sanctuary where thoughts and speeches and books had been fermented. This time, it was not just papers that had been tossed everywhere. Bookcases had been emptied.

"Who on earth?" asked Richard.

"And where is Dad?"

"Pass on both questions. I just don't know," Jackie said.

"We must call the police now," said Richard insistently, puzzled why Jackie had not done this already.

"They will be here soon," said Jackie. "I didn't do it at first because there was no sign of Dad lying dead or anything. And for all I know he may have made it on a trip he was planning."

"And left the place like this? Oh, come on!" exclaimed Richard with a mounting sense of anger at his sister's slowness to act.

"It just that… well, I had a message on my answerphone saying he was OK."

"When was that?" asked Richard.

"Thursday night."

"But this is Saturday," Richard said. "Good God, Jackie, anything could have happened."

"It's all very puzzling," said Jackie. "He was controversial but why anyone should have anything against him enough to kill him just blows me away.

And we just have no proof that he has been murdered or anything", she added.

"Just a room that has been obviously searched and a missing person," Richard groaned.

An obvious question rose in his mind.

"Can this have anything to do with his latest controversy?" he asked. "What's all this about him retracting?" he said. "That doesn't sound a bit like Dad."

"I know," Jackie agreed. She shot an anxious glance at him as the police car drew up.

"This will surprise you. Rumour has it that he had discovered something that shook him to the core. He was inscrutable. But what he said shook me rigid."

"What's that?" asked Richard with surprise as he opened the door to the police.

"It seems he found new evidence for God; a clincher, proof that changed his mind."

To the occupants of the black van drawn up a hundred metres down the street, the conversation they were eavesdropping on had not proved very helpful as yet. The recording devices seemed to be working though.

"When did you find the house like this?" A man's voice was asking.

"This morning, about ten I should say," replied a woman. From the earlier conversation, the occupants of the van knew the voice to belong to Professor Laver's daughter.

So, why had she not raised the alarm immediately after seeing obvious signs of a ransacked house?

"By the way, I'm Sergeant Peter Daniels," the questioner said, introducing himself.

"Well...." There was a pause. "It's just that I had a phone call from Dad on Thursday to say he was all right."

"And why should he want to reassure you on that point?" the Inspector probed.

A pause hung in mid-air.

"I suppose it's the harassment he had been experiencing recently," Jackie replied. "And then I had a phone call from a worried neighbour," she added.

Whatever the Inspector made of that was lost on his eavesdroppers. Either that or thoughts were not clothed with words that they could detect. The voices became a bit muffled as the people in the house were evidently moving from the hallway deeper into the interior.

The bug planted in the professor's study crackled into life.

"How do we know this was no ordinary burglary?" Sergeant Daniels was asking.

"So, where's Dad?" asked a man in exasperation.

"You are Professor Laver's son, I take it?"

"I am indeed," came the reply. "I'm Richard Laver."

"Where's Dad? Well, that is indeed the question," the Inspector said, as the dimensions of the puzzle grew before his eyes.

"You've not heard from him since Thursday night?" he said.

"Neither of us have. As I said," Jackie rejoined. "He had been very anxious recently and wanted to assure me he was ok. I only came down because a neighbour phoned to say he had seen a lot of disturbing things going on but didn't say what."

"And was he in danger?" asked the Inspector. "We'll talk to this neighbour."

"I'm not sure," said Jackie. "He had stirred up a reaction after that item in the Daily Mail and he has never shied away from making strong views - not that anyone would want to kidnap him or anything, I'm sure."

"He was billed as the most celebrated atheist in the word but that's hardly cause for anyone wanting to bump him off," added Richard.

"Unless he was the target of a religious extremist," suggested the Inspector.

"Maybe, so where is he now?" Jackie said, wondering if she should go into details.

"Can we phone him?" suggested the other policeman helpfully.

"No, he didn't take his mobile with him," said Jackie. "He never does, or leaves it turned off or something. He has never quite got the hang of being online all the time."

"But he phoned you from here?" she was asked.

"Oh, yes. I did the 1471 later. It was around 9.30."

"So, he was here on Thursday night but then, when you came to the house this morning, no sign at all." The Inspector was clearly puzzled. It was all very strange.

He would have been even more puzzled if he had noticed his Sergeant filtering through a few drawers hoping to find a piece of paper he was under orders to retrieve. Then he went upstairs, sifting through a waste-paper bin in the computer room. He was greatly relieved to find what he was looking for. Peter Daniels took the piece of paper, folded it and concealed it in his jacket pocket, carefully checking he had not been seen.

"What's all this about Dad changing his whole position?" Richard quizzed Jackie in astonishment, as the Inspector wandered around the downstairs, glancing through papers strewn over any surface going spare. His eyebrows narrowed as he came across something that might just be relevant.

"It seems to be true," Jackie was explaining. "Dad told me he has just uncovered new evidence that seems to demonstrate the existence of God."

"Beyond any reasonable doubt, I suppose," said the Inspector as he came back into the room.

"But that," sputtered Richard, "would be like backing his car down a very long drive he has been motoring up for years! Unbelievable!

What on earth could he have found that suddenly made him do that, for goodness sake?"

"Quite," said Jackie. "And what's it got to do with any of this?"

The occupants of the van listened intently, wondering when the house would yield up its secret. Within a few minutes, Peter Daniels called out from upstairs.

"Sir!" he exclaimed, addressing the Inspector. "You need to see this!"

The Inspector put on a burst of speed and mounted the stairs two at a time, pursued by Richard and Jackie. When they reached the landing, it was not hard to see what it was that had drawn the Inspector upstairs.

In one of the bedrooms, the door of a walk-in had been flung open. Inside was a man, fallen against the shelves, a tall man in his mid-forties, with dark hair matted in small curls. A short beard had flecks of white. But it was the red that drew their eyes down. Congealed blood had dried on his shirt from a gunshot wound to the chest.

The men in the van drawn up down the street exchanged glances. The police had found the body. Silencing their intruder was not part of their brief when they were the intruders. The Director would not be pleased. It would cause unnecessary complications.

As they he been going through Joseph Laver's house the previous night, they hadn't heard him at first. A key had turned in the lock. He had surprised them and there was no alternative. The Director would understand that, even if the police were inevitably to be in involved. One shot through the heart, one practised shot and their intruder was cast into silence. One shot. The Director would be pleased with that at least.

But he was not. On the other side of the world, a man paced the floor in impatience. The operation was not going to plan.

The Director pushed back his hair with his left hand. He was used to ordering the death of anyone who needed to be liquidated. Countless enemies of the State had been rounded up and mysteriously disappeared. Neighbours were left to puzzle, but in the unreality that characterised the atmosphere in which they were compelled to live, no questions asked and no discussion. Disappearance was unexceptional.

But this development was uncalled for. Now the British police were involved and were swarming around the house he had despatched his operatives to the previous day. The police were an unknown factor. The Director could not control them as he would in his own country. But although annoyed, the Director was not unduly alarmed. His operatives would find Joseph Laver before the Press conference he had announced for two weeks ahead. The Professor would not be able to cause trouble.

And the Director's mood became optimistic. The police being involved might even be beneficial. A murder enquiry might even lead his operatives to the Professor and flush him out. He gave instructions to keep listening in and to follow developments.

They heard Jackie scream, a stunned, startled scream that reverberated through the van in which they sat, listening intently. It was not hard to guess what was happening. A man's voice rang out in the gathering dusk.

"That's not Dad!"

The inspector spoke into his mobile phone, calling for immediate support.

"Who the hell is he then?" he asked summarily.

"I've seen him before," Jackie's voice broke the silence. "I think it's a colleague."

"Probably rules out religious extremists being behind all this," observed the Inspector. "If they were targeting your father, why murder someone else? What was the last you heard from your dad?"

"All he said," Jackie said, "was that a week ago, he had a visit from someone else. He didn't say anything about it but I know the visit left him walking about as if he had hot coals under his feet. The next day, he told me he had asked his secretary Julia to book a flight urgently."

"So, he's gone to earth," said Richard.

"Not to earth, no," observed Jackie, forcing a smile despite shaking with shock.

"OK. He said he needed to book a flight to Lima," Jackie replied. "I just hope he's safe as I have no idea if he made it. I've heard nothing more from him since., And now this," she added.

"Peru?" asked Richard with astonishment. And he knew instantly that if his dad was in trouble, he needed to get to him - and quickly.

Whatever might have been said in response to that was lost. Just then, the men listening in the van down the street were startled to hear a phone ring. They were not the only ones to be surprised.

"This doesn't happen every day of the week!" they heard the Inspector exclaim.

The ring tone was coming from the corpse.

Chapter Eight:

A Toyota Flew Down on Top of Him

(Steve's Story)

"So, what happens next?" Jack asked, as the by-now weekly re-zooming session was underway?

"Not sure at this moment," replied Bill with an electronic shrug. "Would anyone like to suggest how my little story unfolds?"

"Could think of several ways the story could go," offered Steve.

"Just like life then!" The yellow marker around the video screen had come from Liam. "Not sure it's all mapped out for us, determined in advance the cast of characters we will meet and what we do."

"Our dad was a rear gunner for a Lancaster when he was twenty," Jack remarked. "He reckoned he was safe until it was his day to go and a German bullet had his name on it!"

"Interesting," Bill said. "He survived though, didn't he? Otherwise, you guys wouldn't be here now."

"He did," said Steve. "He was sent to be a rear gunner because he had learnt to shoot straight aiming at rabbits on our granddad's farm. Ten years after the war, when my Mum died and he married the lady who went on to become Jack's

Mum, he was only just able to speak about his war experiences."

"I remember the one about him cycling round the base when he fell and broke his collar bone," Jack added. "He was grounded. That night, his squadron went on a raid and guess what?"

"His plane got shot down?" Liam volunteered.

"That's exactly what happened," Steve said. "Made him adamant that when it was your time to go, that was your fate!"

"Not sure our lives are mapped out," said Liam. "As a not-so-reverend, I get to see a great many people when I go into the hospital as a Chaplain. Covid is scoring random, countless goals," he added.

"Speaking of which," Steve interjected, "our eight-year-old grandson Peter, mad about football, has drawn himself in goal, stopping the virus getting into goal. Mind you," he added, "playing the sport with his school friends is what he misses most. He's even having his PE classes online. He turns on the laptop camera and copies the teacher's moves. We move the chair and desk as once he fell over!"

"Seems to be quite indiscriminate." The yellow marker made it clear Jack was speaking. "I know some groups in society are getting it worse than others, but this thing strikes anybody down. Doesn't matter what you've done in your life and whether this is payback. It gets anybody and everyone."

"Look, guys," said Steve, moving swiftly on. "Mandy is calling me and I've got to run. But I'd like to offer a story for next week if we're going to be creative."

"This going to be about you?" Jack asked with a casual throwback to the tension that been there for years.

"Not sure how much of me there's going to be," said Steve. "Bill didn't give much away."

And so it was decided. Steve would offer the next piece of creative writing and circulate on email.

It was a night when diamonds lay sparkling on the waters. Flower-sellers plied hotel guests as they sat drinking on the terrace, touched by a warm breeze that caressed and played with them. In every direction, 30-foot high matted date palms spread across the grounds. The moon climbed out of the sea with an orange glow that, at first, barely tipped the gathering night and then slowly rose into a Tunisian evening.

For a while, Wally watched, fascinated, as the moon climbed higher.

It was the first place Wally had ever found that he would want to die in. During the last few troubled months, he had caught himself wondering what it would be like to slip gradually and easily into unconsciousness. When his time came, Wally could think of nowhere he would rather slide away than here on this hotel terrace.

"You like a rose, Monsieur?" enquired a flower boy, standing before him with a white coat, a basket and a cheeky grin.

Wally smiled at him. Last night, he had struck up an acquaintance with this young man, who was studying mathematics by day and in the evenings, sold flowers in the many hotels that lined the beach to raise money for his course.

"Do I look in need of a rose?" Wally asked. Roses were Sharon's favourite flower but he doubted it would keep for the return without becoming faded. The 'rose of Sharon' is what people called her.

The young man tried a different approach.

"To take back to your woman, then!"

"Yes, but which one?" thought Wally.

The flower-seller moved on to another table, leaving Wally with the dilemma that refused to go away. He found himself rattled by the question; disturbed, unable to shrug off his troubled thoughts and settle back to enjoy the softness of evening. Perhaps he would take that cancellation that came up at the meal table earlier on. When offered to him, a two-day safari had seemed an elephant bite out of this idyllic week's holiday, especially when he had promised himself he was getting away to think things over. But Wally wasn't very good at thinking things over. Two days of bare-breasted Germans, two days in which the major decisions were to use the pool or the sea, two days of over-enthusiastic traders were all suddenly enough for him and he chafed at the inactivity.

Now, he noticed what he had not seen before; couples with not much to say to each other and local teenagers looking out at another world. Wally glanced up at the hotel windows.

On the seventh, or was it the sixth floor, a light was turned on and a couple stepped out on to the balcony. Even from that distance, their embrace was mutual and obv**ious.**

Wally felt a sudden pang for what he had lost with Sharon. To think things over, he had returned to the hotel, the scene of a family holiday rich in memories. Not that everything was straightforward then. But this thought jostled for supremacy against another. On a night like this, two years ago in San Francisco, he had waited outside Julia's home, watching with hunger for a sight of her at the window. Then, she had stood at the balcony and Wally knew she had something he wanted.

The arrangements made for the safari, for a while, he paced his own balcony on the ninth floor, restlessly listening to the music that filled the night from the terrace below. He awoke to a red sunrise. It was worth paying a bit extra to connect with this slice of painted creation. If only he could chase the dawn and capture it forever.

The next morning, Wally and his companions were bounced around in the back of a four-wheel drive jeep in a convoy that sped along the coast road. They climbed into the lunar landscape of Matmata, Star Wars country, where ranks of tourists peered curiously into the homes of troglodyte Berber women. Wally was the alien tourist from another world, visiting his own inner country also.

At Zaafrane, on the borders of the Sahara, the group had taken the statutory camel ride, courtesy of the Adhera tribe, who were translating desert skills into experiences that lasted anything from half an hour to eight-day treks for instant nomads.

"I've never experienced such fine soft sand!" someone marvelled, descending from her camel.

"I feel so free," thought Wally. The effect on him was compulsive and instantaneous. For a few minutes, he ran amongst the sand dunes and tumbled down their hot slopes. Dust-like sand trickled luxuriously through toes and fingers.

With heat already building remorselessly, the vehicles swung off the road into open desert. In a few moments, it became clear what their drivers were aiming for. At the crest of a dune stood a row of land-cruisers, white sentinels on a golden landscape. In four-wheel drive country, this was evidently a spot for the tourists to experience the thrills and spills of plunging over the hills of sand.

It was a sequence of images Wally was to record photographically among the corridors of his memory. He had always flipped when death crossed his path. Death had been a taboo subject ever since that fateful day so many years before. Vivid pictures were hung on the walls, immoveable pictures, scenes of fellow travellers bouncing around in wonder and apprehension, of camera-wielding tourists, of local tribespeople hawking sandstone rock carvings and that rollercoaster ride through what seemed to be a clear gap in the ranks of battered land-cruisers and tattered people. But then came the sudden transformation of emotions from pleasure to panic, cries of "watch out for the child", the crunching of gears and brakes, the insufficient turn to the right and the look of horror on a boy's face as a Toyota flew down on top of him.

Passengers screamed and doors flew open. A Bedouin boy lay crumpled and inert on the desert floor. There was nothing anyone could do though everything was tried by the crowd that assembled from amongst the serried ranks of 4 WDs and their occupants. Within two and a half minutes, the life of the Bedouin boy had run into the Sahara.

Suddenly, from amongst the tribespeople standing to one side, a woman emerged. She ran to the lifeless boy and began to wail. Someone in the convoy had a satellite phone. Police and medics were summoned. People stood around listlessly, exchanging impressions. Tourists kept a respectful distance, except for Wally. After a while, moved by a sudden impulse, he went forward to put his hand on the shoulder of the wailing mother. Everyone else looked on in suspense, devoid of the convention that ordinary protocol would dictate. But the woman looked round at Wally. He was confronted by a contorted expression as of someone on a rack, not accepting what had happened. Desperate depths of her eyes drank in comfort from the European who was reaching out to her.

"What's your name?" Wally thought he had asked in his best French.

"Habib." The lips moved.

The moment passed. Other Bedouin were gathering round and so were police vehicles. The jeep was OK. The driver was detained for questioning and a replacement driver sent out. It didn't matter that the safari was called off. No one was in the mood anymore. As if in a funeral procession, the three jeeps drove back to the resorts of the north.

"Habib," exclaimed Wally. "Her name was Habib."

"No," said the guide. "Habib was the name of the boy."

For the next two or three days, Wally walked heavily. He meandered round the souks.

But he couldn't get out of his mind the face of Habib or that of a wailing woman who stared back at him. Wally had always been a survivor, always landed on his feet, always conceived himself to be invincible, possessed of an indestructible quality that gave him mastery of life. But now it bore upon him that life hung by a slender thread. He had never really troubled himself with lonely questions of existence. Life's mysteries were for others to ponder.

But now the need to sort out his own mortality was urgent and pressing. Maybe someday he must seek out the Bedouin woman and express to her his sorrow.

Julia drove back across Golden Gate Bridge, lost in thought. As she neared her home in Marin County, she tried to suppress her pulse from racing in anticipation. Yes, the familiar Mercedes was parked outside. Wally had returned from Tunisia.

"What kept you?" he asked. Then he remembered. "The first Friday of the month. Your ideas group. Are you getting drawn in?"

"Don't be jealous," said Julia as they embraced. "We had a very interesting evening."

"Look, I've only got an hour," said Wally impatiently.

"Then let's make the most of it," said Julia. They went inside. A slow movement ensued between them rather than the passion that sometimes engulfed them. It was a full two hours before Wally got into the Mercedes and drove away. For the hundredth time, Julia felt how much she hated this bit. Invariably, she was sad when it was over. It was always going to be like this. Why had she let him in?

Silicon Valley; a 50-mile corridor running south from San Francisco, the hub of the high-tech revolution. Back in 1957, a group of eight people founded a firm to work exclusively with silicon. It was the California Gold Rush all over again. Almost 40 years on, Silicon Valley was host to 7000 firms. It was the greatest concentrated creation of wealth in all history. A new technology company was going public every five days. 62 millionaires were made every day. Among them was Wally, who had gone to live there after moving from the south of England back in the 1970s. In that autumn of 1996, Wally was not a happy man, ripped apart between a rack of constraints. At one end, his feet were about to be pulled away and set down in the Britain of his boyhood along with his software design company, his family and his wife Sharon. But his heart was being wrenched away towards Julia. There were times when he burned to defy the rationality of common sense that was constraining him to relocate; moments when he wanted to call down curses on doing the right thing and remain. As the time came to re-locate, the burning grew fiercer and louder grew the imprecations.

Meeting her had been a time bomb. It was about to explode in his face and bring destruction. Yet, the alternative was loss of life; his life. Julia had found the secret of what opened him. Instinctively, he knew the key was two-way. Now, Steve sat in the office of his software design company thinking about the growing concern about another time bomb in the system. Ed Yourdon, a programming genius with 24 books to his name, was talking about relocating his family away from New York because on January 1st 2000, he expected it to resemble Beirut.

"What have we created?" Wally asked his Operations Manager.

"It's not looking good," came the reply. "As we cross the threshold into the new millennium, we may be looking at ruined data, airplanes crashing into the sea, Y2K looters roaming the streets, financial stock calculations going kooky, whole systems going down and millions of computers ceasing to exist. It's going to cost hundreds of billions just to fix the endless lines of coded information, never mind clearing up the mess."

General Motors had just closed down one of its automated plants and decided to run a Y2K test before doing so. The clock had been set at December 31st 1999. At the stroke of midnight, the whole factory ground to a halt.

"My buddy says the screen just went blank," said his Operations Manager. "Everything from alarm clocks to power stations could fail; all because the computers don't know what time it is."

"Maybe that's what we do with our lives," wondered Wally to himself. "We're emotional terrorists who place bombs set to detonate and bring the world crashing round about us." "Hey, do I know what time it is?" he said to his Operations Manager, looking suddenly at his watch. It was gone 12.

"There's that guy from Britain speaking at a lunchtime talk. Julia was insistent that I go to hear him."

"You're not getting religious, surely?" asked his Operations Manager. "No, I gave all that up for Lent one year," said Wally flippantly. "I've never thought it made much difference."

Deeper down, the nonchalance was less secure. Until Tunisia, he had regarded himself as a spiritual person without being religious. But now, life was up for grabs.

Wally felt a pang like a toothache for the closeness he had forfeited with his children. Tension between him and Julia over that trial separation three years ago had resulted in their eldest son moving to the UK to live near the British grandparents. Sharon wanted to be near him. Dad was frail and her mother was struggling after her stroke. Wally extending the business to London coincided with a house being built for them on the outskirts of London.

That Sunday, Wally went for a long walk along the seashore at Point Reyes, north of San Francisco. It was a wing-shaped piece of shoreline that once lived near Los Angeles and, like an old beachcomber, had drifted to north California. Francis Drake had landed here. Point Reyes was the epicentre for the earthquake 90 years before that reduced San Francisco to rubble.

In the setting sun of evening, birds soared and danced, flaunting their untrammelled freedom with a boastfulness designed to impress the inhabitants of the flat earth.

Suddenly, Wally felt trapped, yearning to fly upwards and be lost amidst the blue heavens but held fast to the flat earth. Faintly, he heard music play in his inner being. It was a song that called him to soar into the heavens and leave the restrictions of the horizontal world.

But then, a burning log distracted him, the remnant of an earlier picnic on the beach. Steve felt, at that very moment, another pull, the lure of a lady a short drive away. How often had Julia sat before him as they watched a hungry fire consume a log while Wally ran his fingers through her dark curls? Why did forbidden fruit have to taste as sweet as Julia? Attraction, even an affair was one thing! Why did they have to fall deeply in love? It had begun as a helter-skelter of excitement. Then it had gone deep in a way that had got to him profoundly. Wally was resolved. At the earliest opportunity, he would tell Julia that he wasn't going back to Britain. If he couldn't stand the heat, he could always get out of the kitchen.

The man on the rack looked up at the birds mocking him in their soaring gliding movement. Chalk cliffs back-dropped a coastline, wet and windy. This place, epicentre to the 1906 quake, resembled the south coast of England he often walked in during term-time at school before the earthquake came for him. On that occasion, Jerusalem had been the epicentre.

What on earth happened here?" he thought, looking at the scene around him. He shook his head again at the processes that had shaped the landscape. Since birth, the planet had been dented, compressed, eroded, folded, faulted, spilt apart and re-moulded. He knew that the world had not been a peaceful place where landscapes were formed by silent procession. Planet Earth had a violent history, often ripped apart. Titanic forces are struggling for supremacy underneath us; storm battles above and battles beneath, waged under our feet. Awesome powers are on the move.

Wally remembered when he and Julia went to Iceland once. That had been a good holiday. Together, they had witnessed the Earth bleeding with an open wound. Hot lava blood oozed out with a hiss and steam to become one with the wind. New rock was forming. Iceland sat on a seam fissuring the Atlantic all the way down to St Helena. An entire sea floor was broken in two.

Nothing could be relied on. Nothing was firm. But that was also true of the solid ground. As a five-year-old, Wally had looked at an atlas and noticed that South America and Africa fit together like one of his jigsaw puzzles. By then, science was waking up to the weird idea of continents wandering around! That was the day before yesterday. Today, Wally stood on a living world. And still, the birds vaunted and flaunted their gliding freedom as the man on the beach felt a pang for a flat-earth life.

"I wasn't expecting you," Julia said. And she burst into tears.

"What's the matter," asked Wally, "aren't you glad to see me?"

"You just come barging in like that and then you're going to put me down. I'm fed up with being your kept woman. I can't ask you to leave Sharon but I can't go on like this. You'll be back every once in a while, walking through that door as if I was a prize you have come to claim. You can't keep me dangling. I need a life. I've just got to accept you're not going to be a part of it."

"Spending time with you is still the most valuable appointment that goes into my diary," Steve said, instantly realising it was the wrong thing to say.

Julia stormed at this. "I don't want to be an appointment in your diary or anybody's diary. I want... I want to be the most valuable person in somebody's life with no rivals and no competitors. I want to have a relationship I can be proud of openly, like a garden that's the envy of all the neighbours. I want to be loved!" she shouted through her tears.

"I love you more than I know how to say," said Wally tenderly.

"I know you do," said Julia as the storm abated. "And I feel like that way too. But I need a permanent relationship, someone who to me will be an oasis, not a mirage."

They held each other tightly, eyes blinded with tears. Wally wept. It was the first time he had wept openly since Jerusalem. Something broke in him. Julia responded to his vulnerability, aware that this man was giving her something that was incredibly rare and therefore valuable. They found the bedroom. She said it was the last time. Urgency and tempestuous passion erupted until words and thoughts were drowned in a heaving sea.

When it was all over, Wally persuaded her to meet one other time before the flight to Britain. Staunch sanity returning, Julia was adamant. Their relationship had gone as far as it could. Then she relented. He could come before Christmas to say goodbye.

Wally did not return. The day before Christmas, he and Sharon drove to say goodbye to Sharon's brother David. Wally was intending to leave her there for a while and then find some pretext to slip away. He craved for Julia. Sharon was sweet and lovely but she was not a warm person. Her mother was not a warm person. Her mother's mother had not been a warm person. But Julia was different.

"What's she got that I haven't got?" asked Sharon suddenly, as they turned off the interstate highway. There was no rancour, no explosion, just a quiet voice; "What's Julia got that I haven't got?"

Sharon had seen them out together once, though they had no idea they were being watched. From the way they held hands, laughed and looked at each other, she knew with unsubtle intuition that Wally loved the other woman. A rough and tumble between the sheets was one thing. This was far worse. Slack-jawed disbelief led to an explosive concoction of tears and anger. Ever since, Sharon's life had been on hold, waiting for something to happen. She couldn't settle into anything. Uncertainty drained the colour off the walls and painted her room with uneven colours. Often, Sharon convinced herself that she was entirely to blame. Other times, she declared independence of him and asserted her freedom to get on with life without him. But today heard only a quiet voice.

It reached him as nothing else could. Wally drove on in silence. He felt wretched and split, as if the inquisition had been working on him.

"What do you see in her?" repeated Sharon.

"Don't say that, Sharon," pleaded Wally.

Then Wally added, though he wished he could pull his words back even as they sprang out of his mouth, a collection of deadly daggers, "I've met someone who listens to me, who notices me. It's as simple as that. You haven't noticed me for a long time."

"You're telling me you've fallen in love with someone and it's my fault?" Sharon was indignant.

"No. Of course not. I'm to blame too. I haven't valued you as I ought. Julia gives me something."

"Do you remember that beautiful book you gave me?" asked Sharon after a while. "It was an antique book about Old England. That's how you treated me then, a book gift-wrapped and to be treasured, open especially for you," said Sharon through her tears. "But now, you want me on your mantlepiece, sometimes admired but rarely touched. I don't want to gather dust. I want to be taken down."

And she cried for the loneliness of being unread.

Wally reached out to comfort her. At first, he didn't notice the girls running into the road. Then he did. He swerved. A lorry was coming from the opposite direction. There was no chance to swerve a second time. The vehicles collided with a combined speed of 120 miles an hour. Nothing could have been more unexpected. One moment, a man was reaching out to comfort his stricken wife. Then, this great object had appeared from nowhere and blotted everything out, carrying them down the slope. In slow motion, Wally watched. Then the world stopped spinning.

For ten minutes, the world stopped spinning. Wally and Sharon were stunned into semi-consciousness, blood pouring from a dozen cuts from a shattered windscreen. For ten minutes they sat, unable to move, pinned by the wreckage. But their eyes could move. Each saw blood pouring from the other. Each of them thought the other must be dead. Both were wrong.

It took an hour for firemen to cut them out of the wreckage. Wally and Sharon sat, trapped. They didn't attempt speech. No words would form themselves and leap from their cut lips; only thoughts, unexpressed and unformed. But Wally was sick at heart. Sometimes, he had hoped Sharon might resolve his dilemma by conveniently passing away. Then she could be the honoured dead, a martyr to his cause, attended with flowers and devoutly spoken of and wrapped in whispered memory.

But all that was now gone. Wally sat there watching his own thoughts take shape from his brain. In that wreckage, a detached emotional retina was jolted back into position. Though he could see little of Sharon beyond a sideway's glance from a trapped head, in his mind's eye, suddenly he could see all of her. She looked beautiful to him again and he realised how much he did love her. He would give anything to have her back, to take that book down once more from the shelf and to start from page 24 or wherever he had left off.

Blood was oozing from his polo sport pique through the zip jacket that would be khaki no longer. Sharon could just turn her head enough to see that much. Wally had been a great guy. Despite everything, she loved him fondly. Once, they were soul mates. Then their souls changed. Now, Sharon would never be read. And she couldn't feel her left leg.

While both were thinking of each other in the past tense, someone (they never knew who) moaned softly. Even as they were being cut out, they received each other as back from the dead.

When it was all over, they talked long into the night.

Within a few weeks, Julia's friends said she was smiling with a secret confidence. She was pregnant.

Chapter Nine:

A Tale of Two Poets

Contemporary culture anaesthetises anything to do with tragedy or trauma into banal superficiality where everything is fun. And then came Covid; the minute enemy that ripped through the planet. The scars would last a long time. The economic shock was both deep and dramatic. Experts warned that the world is likely to face a global crisis in poor mental health after the pandemic has passed.

Pandemics tend to magnify existing inequalities rather than flatten them. The most affluent managed to shelter, hide from the virus in their gardens or second homes, work remotely and get food delivered to their homes courtesy of Deliveroo and online slots. Poverty made the experience of Covid harder to bear. It was the lower-paid working communities that were harder hit, often cramped in tower blocks and homes without gardens. Plus, of course, the elderly and vulnerable. There was an inter-generational as well as class divide. Resilience depends on capacity. How people fared in that public health emergency was a very different experience, according to social location.

We were navigating the same sea but in very different boats.

Through the late Spring, the deadly virus wrought its work, restlessly looking for new victims to infect. Despite all best efforts to clamp it down, the invisible enemy deposited itself into unsuspecting carriers, crawling up the nose and silently hijacking the means to draw living breath. It consumed before it destroyed, thence to be passed on to someone, anyone who was available. Or would it be a dead-end destiny? Like rabies, it would infect one person and go no further. As it spread across the anxious globe, Covid was mutating, replicating and adding new branches to its family tree. Maybe its passage through humans caused it to weaken. The contagion would give up the fight if humanity was a dead-end host. No one knew though global teams raced against the clock to find an answer.

What could the human race do to combat this genetic strip of instructions whose purpose is to replicate itself? We tried soap. That was effective enough on the skin, washing its way through the layer of fat that encased the lethal enemy. The genetic guts of the virus spilled out. But war by soap was not enough. Inside our bodies, the task was much harder. Governments dusted down a well-researched playbook for how to deal with a pandemic, starting at Chapter One. Others were slow to react and paid for it later. The world was working together at the technical level and the scientific level with much tracing and co-operation across borders between researchers. The world was not working so well at the political level, bolting down the hatches and trading geopolitical accusations. It was a happy hunting ground for conspiracy theorists always on the lookout for a cover-up, a plot or an accident that went wrong.

Care homes represented war in the trenches. Care homes suffered some of the most severe outbreaks of Covid-19 in the country. The equivalent of three per cent of the total capacity of care homes in England and Wales had, by now, lost their lives to Covid-19. In some areas of London, the number was as high as fifteen deaths for every 100 beds.

That included Bill's uncle Len. Bill heard the news one Thursday evening, just having stepped back in from the weekly ritual of clapping health care workers to cheer them on and be a national megaphone for thanks. What disturbed him about the phone call was not only to hear that this 95-year-old warrior had lost his fight, it was that a Filipino member of staff, who had taken particular interest in him and nursed Len faithfully, had also succumbed to the biological mockery. Kach died without family or friends near her after spending more than two weeks in intensive care. Bill remembered her as a very gentle, caring, family-oriented person who loved her daughter more than anything. The Care home manager said that Kach had started feeling unwell with a cough and began struggling to breathe towards the end of the month. An ambulance took her to hospital. When Kach was about to go in the ambulance, she was crying and pleading with her friend to please look after her daughter. It was so heartbreaking. Kach knew it was the last time she'd see her.

Bill was distraught with misty eyes that became a torrent of long-lived emotion. His mum's death was the first time he could remember crying. But he had cried when he and his father were united in grief after Micky was killed in Vietnam. Bill loved the tree-climbing cousin companion of his youth.

News had come through that Micky was missing in action, presumed dead. For three days, ordinary household sounds jarred like the inside of a tomb. Every time the phone rang, their nerves hung taut, like a cat bracing itself for danger. Then came the missile under their front door. "I regret to have to inform you...Michael Trimble died of wounds in Cambodia two days ago". 15 months later, there was a knock at the door from a one-armed man. It was Micky's friend Jay, come to tell Len Trimble how his son had met his death, caught on patrol in an incursion into Cambodia.

A few harmless shots had greeted the patrol as it crossed the border, but it met no real opposition. Vietcong scrambled out from one village and were promptly killed by rifle fire. Heat and tiredness numbed Micky to the blank fear he often felt. The patrol was jumpy, taking no chances. Two boys were looking over the wall at the unusual sight of GI's tramping by. It was better to fire first and ask questions when slightly more convenient. With the wantonness of a boy destroying some harmless bird just for sport, Micky fired. The boys ran off. Micky wondered what war was doing to them all. He had just contributed his share to man's inhumanity to man.

In the next village, they were offered rice and a kind of cake by an old woman. In the dust track that passed for a street, they could see people staring. Others began to run away and dive into doorways. In a clearing nearby, it was an effort to sleep that night. Micky's life of ease made it difficult to sleep soundly under those conditions. He lay awake smelling the jungle. It was not unlike the smell of the forest back home after a fall of rain. The next day, not far from the village, they found themselves in the middle of heavy shelling. The colonel, phlegmatic as always, asked for two volunteers to work out where the enemy was. Their position was untenable. Micky and Jay were chosen. They puffed and panted their way to the top of a hill that afforded an excellent view of the enemy's position.

They reached the top of the hill before realising, too late, that they were surrounded. It was a fight between man and the primaeval forest. Despite there being no one there, a brisk and deadly exchange took place. The firing from semi-automatics was intense. Ammunition was running short. Micky was hit. His groin was transformed into a bloodstain with crimson bubbles. With one arm blown off at the elbow, Jay crawled out in an attempt to get out of there. The ghosts of the trees became shapes of people with guns, shapes that were coming nearer. Micky scored two direct hits at a distance of ten yards. But the end was coming nearer too. For a few more minutes, the air around him sang with machine-gun bullets. Then came that deep silence that descends on a battlefield when the victors have won. Just then, the shadow of a plane swept like a ghostly hand over the scene, the shadow of an F4 Phantom called in to provide air support. With a few bursts of cannon, the enemy became spirits of the trees once more. Micky's body was recovered. Jay was still alive, watching, in disbelief, an arm that now finished at the elbow.

Bill could remember as if it were yesterday, Uncle Len drinking all this in. It was a cruelly confusing drink, laced by the evenings of harrowing pain through which he had passed, but mixed with quiet pride. Len Trimble was still dimly wondering how he would live out the weary days that remained to him, days of Good Friday without Easter. And Bill wept that Mick would never again hear the sound of crickets in the forest near their home or smell the trees and the grass after a fall of rain.

It was the new Spielberg blockbuster that triggered emotions still tender when he confided in Beth what was going on inside. 'Saving Private Ryan'. An American soldier trapped in a combat zone fighting a versatile enemy in hostile terrain. That's what had happened to Micky, except he wasn't rescued in time. He wrote to Beth to tell her Len had succumbed. First, he would tell Katie. Uncle Len had been somewhat of a grandfather figure to Katie.

Except he couldn't bring himself to. Bill opened the front door. It was clear that Katie was in love.

After the clapping had subsided and the neighbours retreated once again into domestic incarceration, Katie lingered. Then she saw him again. Robert Morrison had been back late from work now that limited resumption of business was being allowed. As soon as the Volvo swung into the drive opposite, he appeared, looking sharp despite the absence of pin-striped suit. Neither was sure who started it, but one mention of balcony-singing Italians was enough.

A few lines of Rigoletto were all they could muster. But in the delightful dusk, 'Some Enchanted Evening' seemed very fitting (and somewhat easier!) Rogers and Hammerstein oscillated across the street. Robert held forth, then Katie. And Robert brought up the rear. "Once you have found her, never let her go," he sang. The two singers offered a repeat performance and the concert was done.

When she came in later, Bill told her about Uncle Len, who had been like a father to him at one point when his own Dad opted out of life after Mum's cancer. Katie's enigmatic smile changed in an instant. She gave Bill a big hug that went on for a while.

"So pleased you're finding some happiness," he said.

"I don't know," Katie parried. "I guess there will be lots of lockdown love, but see how it goes. Can I be totally honest, Dad?" she asked tentatively.

"Of course," Bill said, giving her permission though wondering what was coming.

"Well, you know that story you did, that you shared amongst your friends? It's very interesting and all that, but there's not much of you in it."

"Does there have to be?" wondered Bill, as they tucked into supper. "It's a mystery story."

"I get that," said Katie. "But you yourself were in the position of that Professor at one time, you told me. I would have thought it would be interesting to make it first person. My real problem, though, is with Steve's story. Nice try to deflect to someone else, a third person. But like your story, where is the voice of the author? Steve's story just doesn't add up. It's just too much 'happy ever after.' From what I gather from these old letters, he went back to Beth afterwards. At some point, he made her pregnant."

"That's a very interesting statement!" Bill exclaimed. Katie had done an English literature degree and Bill's respect for her suddenly mushroomed. An hour later, Beth's reply came in.

My dear friend (came a reply that night as his Smart Phone pinged),

I'm so, so sorry to hear of Uncle Len's passing. There have been numbers of tragedies that have marked both our lives and so I join you this evening (your time), in the resonance of the grieving.

Every soul is unique, made as I have come to believe, in the image of God. For us, there will never be another Len Trimble outside of the resurrection to come. He has lived his days now but for me, it is the resurrection rather than some vague idea of an after-life that sets the seal on hope.

What a huge amount of loss everyone is going through right now. In New York City we've had several hundred thousand cases and over 16,000 deaths. Today was the first day we've had no fatalities. So, what gets us through in such a severe shock? Intervention using the firepower of a modern State, for one; dedication of those in the care professions, for another. Then there was social solidarity invoking enormous kindness. But there was, as well, the remarkable charismatic personalities of cities and communities, like the firemen who clapped the health workers. Or the faith communities reaching out in tandem with mutual aid groups that multiplied everywhere but also had their own resource of hope based on another world.

Just as the pandemic may be weakening at last, up comes sickening awareness of the virus in the mind. The horrific last words of George Floyd – 'I can't breathe' – underline the Coronavirus that saps the lungs. But it also shows the way our system suffocates the value of each life. That came home to me last year when I invited a friend from the UK to dinner here. David grew up with racist language and discrimination but was still not prepared for what happened when he arrived at the apartment lobby carrying a bag with a bottle and some flowers. The front desk led him to me through an open courtyard to the back of the building, past residents' garbage bags and into a dirty lift. It seems the doorman thought he must be a delivery guy and made him use the service elevator. It's those lazy assumptions that are as pernicious as the outright racism and disregard of life. The central assumption is that there are different levels of worth - a hierarchy of lives. We've got to get rid of it.

I'm off to march in a few minutes but just wanted to say it's not just that Black Lives Matter. The elderly matter and need looking after as well. We don't see only the resonance of those who have swum in the sea of grief; we can find resonance between our different selves. The loss you feel with Lenny will bring back the memory of your cousin. It may also have some echo with that night you saved me when I was coming apart at the seams. Speaking of which, I don't see why I shouldn't share with you the lines of verse I wrote to try to express what was going on. So here it is.

That far off night, Beth thought of the child growing inside her. The child would be safe; never have to be raised in a world of sandpapered edges.

But the bleeding returned; a thin red line that haunted her. Why was her own body doing this to her? Didn't it know she wanted this child? She wanted to scream at her own body as if it was blindly following a programme that must be halted immediately. But the next day, the doctor was grim.

"I'm afraid that unless the bleeding stabilises, the prognosis is not good."

"Not good?" she repeated in disbelief.

Two days of bed-rest followed. On the third day, the bleeding returned strongly and they confirmed the miscarriage. Beth had a D&C and was then allowed to go home.

Bill was there waiting for her with a bunch of roses. They embraced but no tears flowed. "Even in distress, she's dignified," he thought. Then she wept quietly, accepting without words the tissues he extracted from the box in her kitchen. After a few moments, Beth regained a semblance of composure.

"The baby's gone," she said without emotion. He left after a while, shutting the door on a woman whose inner being was disintegrating.

"I'm being punished," thought the lady on the demolition site. "I wanted to cheat him. I should never have tried to keep a permanent part of Steve."

She tried to place a call to Steve's office to tell him. His secretary promised to tell him she had phoned, noting that her voice sounded wobbly and tired. Then, Beth dissolved into tears, weeping for the child that would never know life. Her grief would have been painful to witness if there were any witnesses.

Throughout that long night, images kept blurring together like slide projector images on the wall of her memory. Flashes, dimly formed, were gone, hauntingly, before she could get a fix. As she struggled to sleep, she remembered long ago nights of elusive sleep when she had been too terrified to close her eyes.

Recurring nightmares began to form a pattern. There were hands over her face and then her body, a dark shadow of a stranger whose face she fought to recognise. Beth sat up, panting heavily, her stomach knotted as the dark images leered out of the shadows and stood to attention.

It was her father! Dark secrets in a darkened room arose from under the sheets, skeletons shaking their chains in her face, mocking her. Blanked out horrors of what her father did when they were alone rose up from nowhere. Beth saw as a spectator, watching with fascinated objectivity, watching in slow motion forgotten memories of being a wife substitute for her father, who came to her most nights.

What was this? What on earth was going on? She dimly realised that the miscarriage must have triggered memories long suppressed. One child dying who had lived. Another child coming back to life who had long since been dead. Coming back to life on the third day. Dark secrets in a darkened room.

Beth couldn't remember crying before she was 12. In fact, a full year of her life had been ripped from her memory. So it was amnesia then, the amnesia that stops people going insane. She had done anything rather than feel the pain. Was this why she had gone numb, losing touch with her feelings just when she wanted to enjoy herself? Beth became an expert at avoiding these memories. Amidst a surfeit of gathering memories, she took her pen and began to write down what she was feeling. A latent poet had been waiting for this moment to be born.

> *"Come and see the innocent child".*
> *Once blissfully unaware,*
> *Her youth betrayed*
> *By one she trusted,*
> *Now there is guilt. Shame.*
> *Where once there was calm.*
> *Dreams shattered,*
> *Childhood destroyed.*
> *Smother the pain*

To hide its reality.
A layered mask
To face the world,
Unchained memory
Buried deep inside.
Child made woman
Against her will.

No wonder she had been soiled for life. It was for this, then, that she had maintained a dignified reserve. She lived her life within rigid layers of self-protection. Beth sobbed for herself and for the child within her that had faded away. The floor continued to fall. Mysteriously, two images were blending, blurring, melding. She saw two children, one the reality of what had now died within her, and another, a forgotten ghost from a forgotten past. Deep within her anguished psyche, a change took place that night that mirrored what was going on in her body. Two children were changing places. The forgotten ghost was becoming a real child as the real child joined the world of ghosts. On and on into the night she wrote.

"The icy hand of fear grips my heart,
Making every beat a cry of pain.
Helplessly I watch
As you fade away before my eyes;
It was yesterday.
The pains that brought you forth,
The answer to so many prayers.
The sound of your laughter

The wonder in your eyes
Once bright, now clouded,
Carrying the weight
Of overmuch sorrow
In so young a frame.
How did I do this?
Become the cause of wounds so deep?
Your fragile dreams shattered
In ruins
Round my feet.

A week had passed since the miscarriage and the shock discovery. Beth took up a worn pen, compelled to express emotions that refused to die. She treasured that pen. The Christmas present from Steve was all she had of him now. Her vitality had emigrated. A drained, strained face, gaunt and lined with pain, greeted Bill whenever he came by. Beth sat for hours looking at the view across the hills from her home. Not even the riot of colour could raise her depressed spirits. Since getting in touch with her inner pain, she had never felt so acutely the wilderness desolation of things.

The tunnel, a whirlpool,
Draws me to its centre,
Leaving behind the agony.
Perspectives distorted
By images of the mind.

The darkness is cold,
Numbing my aching senses.

Shall I relinquish life,
Drown without trace?

I have a choice
Standing on the edge;
Withdraw from the hurt
Cutting off the pain
A living vacuum
Alone
I cannot live without love
I would not hurt
If I had not loved.
If I love again
I am vulnerable
Again

Shall I take faltering steps
Away from the tunnel
And build my life
Out of shattered ruins
Of what once was?

Beth had allowed Katie to see the poetry. They were close and had been from bewildered babyhood.

"Still think Steve's story doesn't add up?" Bill asked her the next evening.

"Even more so!" said Katie emphatically.

"Look at this letter from Mandy in your batch of old papers. Trying to piece things together, she clearly confided in you after they had returned to the UK. I know you had been friends, but remember this? I'm jumping straight into the relevant part.

Dear Bill,

At times, every nerve in my injured leg reveals its identity. I now walk through life in a chair. But better to damage a leg than lose a life. I have one good leg. And a good job. I enjoy my work. The menu before a human rights lawyer certainly has variety.

What was it that Bosnian woman pleaded with her? 'Tell someone that we are worth fighting for. We are people, not animals for the slaughter or dogs for their sport'." But though the woman's life and dignity had been ripped up along with her clothing, amazingly, she was not bitter or even held animosity towards her tormentors. Forgiveness? I couldn't do it. That's asking too much.

I keep thinking of how Steve had left me like an old discarded vase by his affair with Beth and his refusal to admit there was anything going on. I don't have hard evidence that would pass muster in a court of law, but recently, there have been a number of furtive conversations I have caught in the breeze when passing by Steve's study; the phone calls when there was no one on the other end, the change in his voice when he mentions San Francisco. Whispered conversations along a hall rose up to mock here, ghosts laughing along the corridor. Despite him laying it on thick that the business trips were both a chore and a bore, I know Steve enough to sense a thin disguise. He is almost certainly seeing Beth again, or at least playing with the romance. Since the accident, Steve had been trying hard. But so many words rose up to taunt her and the axe marks on her spirit felt worse than ever. Forgiveness? Never. I have no wish to recover from being replaced.

It happened again this evening. Your mutual friend Liam had come to look us up. The way I figure it, while he and I were deep in conversation, now was a good time to phone Beth again. Once or twice a month, he found a time and place for a furtive conversation. Transatlantic intimacy gave fresh colour to romantic images that seemed to be painted forever on the walls of his memory. They were a part of him. Slowly, he dialled familiar numbers. But there was no reply. Steve hung on for a few minutes, propping up his emotions. I picture the scene like this as it wasn't long before he rejoined us.

I take the liberty of sending you something I wrote recently only so you can see the depths of my feelings. If you can just find out from Beth if there is anything going on, please ask her to stop.

I just hope I'm wrong. Now to get lunch. Until last autumn, I staunchly maintained that choosing, preparing and eating food were among the most civilised pleasures on offer anywhere in the world. Since the accident, my world has been a valley, or at best, a flat earth. Now some hills of interest are slowly forming. Despite my suspicions, for the first time for months, I'm enjoying cooking.

In Britain, a writer is writing out her private sense of betrayal and weary, weary emotions.

"God, I'm tired.
I've so tried so hard
To make right choices
To put the past behind;
God, I'm tired
Of being everything to everyone.
It's lonely in here.
An endless struggle
To run a house
Go to work
Be there for the children
Superwoman
I can't anymore.
Eaten away
Piece by piece
Nothing left
Unrelenting torture
Hideous scenes replay
Uninvited thoughts drop by
Tormenters of the day and night
Elusive freedom
Temptation to end it all
Permanently

In Britain, the writer comes to an end by the first light of morning.

But for the writer in San Francisco, there would be no respite.

"Yes, he came back to her," admitted Bill. "It was to say a proper goodbye – or so he said. That part of his story is 'happy ever after'. You would need to change it. In his narrative, Julia becomes pregnant later. So, it is definitely not a neat, tidy closure."

"Self-serving narrative I would say," concluded Katie. "The guy is wrapping it up as if he lives in a romantic novel. It's bloody Mills and Boon."

"But you loved her yourself, didn't you? How you stuck with her through the miscarriage and have remained close from as long as I can remember."

Bill nodded. Once again his eyes misted over and then the dam burst.

"I saved her," he said after a while.

"Of course I loved her. In a different universe, Beth would have made a tremendous wife. Her sociable, gracious manner was an unfailing invitation to put me at ease. But I would have to reckon that, in Beth's life, relationships were a place you passed through without stopping. Whenever anyone had got close, Beth backed off. It would be a special person she would allow into the inner sanctum, rather than just a foot in the door. Why Steve was so privileged I would never know.

"One Friday, I had the strongest urge to call on Beth. I hadn't heard from her for a while. The answerphone wasn't on but neither was she responding. That wasn't like her. I couldn't resist the impression that I should go over there. These days, I kept her spare key in case she locked herself out. As I drew up outside the familiar home, I could see there was light on inside somewhere but not in the porch. Beth must be out. Disturbed, I decided to settle down to wait for her return. I couldn't see what was going on inside the house.

It was Friday evening and Beth Johnson was cutting off her long black hair. Thursday evening was the night when the phone had not rung. She was resolved to be out when Saturday evening arrived.

Beth watched as if in slow motion, each piece of hair taking its time to dance to the floor. Black shards of broken dreams lay around her, caught in the soft green-yellow light of her dressing table as her hair began to form dark patterns on the carpet. Steve had loved to put his hand through her hair, caressing its silkiness. He wouldn't do that anymore. With Steve, it was not a little piece of her but a total sacrifice dragged with initial reluctance and then with full-hearted enthusiasm to the altar. This evening, there was nothing left; sacrifice consumed, awaiting consummation.

Beth looked out of the window, watching a grey sky that clung tenaciously to the restless contours of San Francisco Bay. At last, she was to escape from the swirling mist. 'I won't make it to the year 2000 now', she thought. Beth was impaled on retribution. Her father stood as a conspirator over her, demanding a ransom. That, she knew full well, was why emotions about Steve were so tangled.

When she was young, the family home they occupied near the San Andreas fault line had sometimes rumbled, the stomach of the earth belching in curious synchronicity with Dad's ugly moods. More recently, it had taken three months for her personal tremors to fall silent after the miscarriage and the trauma of recovered memories. But the tremors now rested in the earth and nothing was left standing.

And now, it was late Friday night and Beth wore the kimono that Steve liked so much. When they found her, that would be a final message to him. As the last piece of black hair fell tauntingly to the ground, she opened the tube of killers, gulped down 40 and lay on the bed waiting. Beth took a final lingering farewell of the sunset as her world was swallowed up by night. The light slowly faded and the last recollection she had was looking into the face of Steve. Steve, or was it Bill? What was he doing here? It was a dream, a final mockery, she decided, as she slipped into the whirlpool and down a long tunnel of beckoning sleep that whispered to her.

Chapter Ten:

The Day Had Begun Slowly and Without Drama (Jack's Story)

Katie's life had begun with drama and then flowed more slowly.

Bill was never quite sure how much the loss of Ali had affected her, beyond the obvious withdrawal of the ever-present Great Mum figure, imposing and warmly encompassing. God knew he had done his best to raise her as his own deeply loved daughter, the 'what might have been daughter' if he and Ali had got together. He had loved this little black girl as his own soul. Many were the days of babyhood when he had cradled her and they spent long hours peering into each other's eyes.

Uncle Len had performed valuable service as a surrogate grandfather and for that, he would be forever grateful. It pained him now that he couldn't even go to the funeral with Katie. What was it that she had said to him earlier when they watched the protests demanding racial justice on the news?

"You know, Dad, this moment is so very powerful. It feels like a lot of history is going on right now. George Floyd didn't deserve to die. An unarmed black man! All for twenty dollars," Katie said angrily.

"Looking back, love, how much prejudice do you think you faced at school and here in the UK?" Bill enquired. It was not a subject they usually discussed. Katie was deliberate but poignant.

"The only way I can describe it," she said, "is that there were times when I felt like an alien. Behind closed doors or when the teacher had left the room, there was this stupid idiot who called me the 'n' word. Others asked if I could speak English. When I was learning the flute, some looked me as if to say, 'why you doing this?' My face didn't fit, clearly. The problem is so deep-rooted in society that you can't escape it."

"You never told me all that!" Bill exclaimed. "Wish I'd known," he lamented. "Why didn't you tell me!? Think things will change as a result of the black lives movement and all these protests?"

"Truly don't know," Katie said. "A good friend of mine was arrested last year for arson for no good reason. He gets stopped and searched twice a year. It's the unconscious bias. That way, treating people as being lesser value has to work itself out through shock awareness, maybe. Don't worry; all that cover stuff that went on at school. The video of George Floyd triggered a whole lot of stuff in me. But look," she said, changing the subject as she saw it distressed Bill, "What's the latest story?"

"It's from Jack," said Bill, still reeling from what she had just shared with him. "You can read it."

The day had begun slowly and without drama. The eastern sky had allowed a few shafts of sunlight to penetrate its inky blackness before yielding itself to the inevitable. But the surrender had been measured and the day did not abandon itself to the morning; greyness hung over the world until the day was a few hours old. Then came the moment of joyful surrender, the dissipation of dullness and the proud announcement of a blue sky.

"The sun is going to come out after all," remarked my host as we sat and breakfasted together. Sure enough, the sun was already bathing the day in warmth. Even at that time in the morning, the oven temperature must have been set high. With the triumph of blue and yellow complete, nothing could stop the warmth escalating into a heat with a dominance that would be inescapable.

"It's going to be a hot one!" said Miguel again. It was a day that threatened ferocity.

Uruapan lay in the west central highlands of Mexico. When the Spanish monk, Fray Juan de San Miguel, came here in 1533, so struck was he by the River Cupatitzio and the lush vegetation it watered that he called the area Uruapan, 'fruit and flowers' or 'eternal spring'. Now the land of fruit and flowers had grown into a thriving city of 200,000; a centre for the many farms that filled the district. Uruapan was renowned for the quality and size of its avocados. An annual fair celebrated the avocados, a fair that was incomplete without its regular bullfights.

The city had a strange attraction for me. I remembered the time as a young twenty-two-year-old traveller, I had visited the volcano at Paricutin, 35 kilometres to the west. One February afternoon in 1943, an Indian farmer, Dionisio Pulido, had been ploughing his cornfield. Suddenly, the ground was swelling, shaking, swelling and roaring steam dust. Within a year, a volcano had risen above the surrounding land, now buried in a sea of black, solidified lava. To this day, the church tower in the old village of San Juan still peered uneasily above the black lava sea; a mute survivor of the day the Earth bulged and hissed.

At the bar of the Hotel Villa Flores, a colonial-style hotel west of the central plaza, I had met Miguel, son of an avocado farmer who knew everything about Paracutin. Miguel had invited me to stay at their house. It had led to a firm friendship between me and Miguel. Over the years, I had visited a few times.

The heat had demanded of everyone that they lie down and enjoy their siesta. It was not till late in the afternoon that I ventured out again. By then, the calm breeze was breaking thermal dominance, emancipating its prisoners and touching the senses with delight.

The wind blew mysteriously, sovereignly, gently. It rose from a point that was neither fixed nor obvious. Where it stopped or ended, no one could tell. Down in the valley, we could see smog arising from vehicle exhausts. Nearby, construction workers had just completed the preparation for the demolition of a building. Suddenly, it toppled, enveloping the scene with clouds of dust. Miguel had been painting in a bedroom in his house that day and the windows had been open. A patient atmosphere absorbed all these fumes and smells, preparing to restore freshness to the world in exchange.

That evening, Miguel, his wife Juanita, their son and me sat eating on the verandah. Tacos, quesadillas, burritos, enchiladas – all the usual things were there in abundance, plus a Mexican cocktail I don't believe had made my acquaintance before. Miguel was in his mid-forties, a thin man with a beard and a stonewashed denim jacket under which he sported a shirt with a Granddad-style collar. He said very little, only half-listening to the conversation between me and his wife, reminiscing in comprehensible Spanish about the day when electricity hummed into their farm, courtesy of magic wires.

"Before electricity transformed our lives, the windmill was the main source of power on our farm. Now we are putting windmills up again. Green power will soon be taking over!"

Pausing between bites of enchilada, I smiled. "Maybe, like the windmills, we've come full circle," he said, smiling. "Until recent times, ships relied on harnessing the gift of the wind. Not like the ships I sailed on, of course."

Now he had proved he was alive, Miguel would not be silent. "Sometimes," he said, "when I lie awake listening to the wind beating against the ship, I try to imagine a world without wind. How dry and airless it would be."

Juanita clapped her hands." Ah, I have imagined that too," she said.

"Definitely," I concurred. "Without the wind, a smell would last a hundred years. Dust from a falling building or fumes from a painted room would linger long in a fusty, musty world." The combination of English words sounded slightly odd through the sieve of my poor Spanish accent. "The wind brings the world to life."

Miguel glanced at me as he said this. There was clearly something to him, an imagination that wanted to soar into the skies.

"Where have you been working these past few years?" Juanita was curious.

"I have been a Radio Officer on board ships of various kinds," I explained.

"What kind of places have you visited?"

A smile curled on my lips.

"I have worked everywhere, across the world," I said. "Tramp steamers, cargo vessels and finally P & O on the cruise liners. I enjoyed that most. I never seemed to stay in one regular job for very long, though."

I guess my words were a Morse code for what I had no wish to reveal to these casual acquaintances. Maybe I could have told the story of a restless soul, blown hither and thither by the wind, an unsolid, immaterial existence, ephemeral and ghostly. The pain of a lost relationship with my Dad rustled fleetingly in my memory. Then an image of a little boy gazing wistfully at his younger brother, preferred by his father's second marriage. Even at school, I would work my long socks off and obtain the best reports I was capable of.

It was all to no avail. In my own eyes, I never felt I measured up. That feeling was a ghost which my father had commanded to walk the painful corridors of my mind. 30 years later, the ghost still walked. I was no nearer feeling that I measured up and I cursed myself because I knew I still craved for recognition from a father now old and frail.

"I expect you had interesting experiences," said Juanita as she brought in the next course.

"Yes, I certainly did," I agreed. My thoughts wandered back over two years to a message received from the San Francisco Police Department for a passenger on board. The passenger's wife had died in a freeway pile-up. I thought that name sounded familiar from school days. Trimble had come to the radio room to send messages to make arrangements to leave as soon as possible and fly home. I recognised the modest-looking man immediately, though a quarter of a century stood unbending since their last meeting.

"Bill Trimble! Well, as I live and breathe! After all these years!"

We had shaken hands. Remembering the sudden bereavement that had brought them together, I felt awkward, unsure of what to say. I hadn't seen my old school friend for a generation. Not, in fact, since that incident in Jerusalem after which Bill had returned to California.

But now, rather than allow the chain of memories to pull too much to the surface, I changed direction quickly, tacking like an old ship of sail. So, we talked about the changeable winds and the atmosphere that moved above them.

Suddenly, thunder shook the house. Lightning forked in massive surges of electricity, a display of raw power combined with a vibrating, jagged voice.

"It always surprises me," I said as we sat on the covered verandah watching the storm, "that the atmosphere is so thin. You could drive up through it in an hour. Listen to all that fighting going on right now in the lowest layer. Do you know, across the world, there are 2000 thunderstorms in progress at any time?"

"That is a lot of power, signor?" enquired Miguel's son in broken English.

"It certainly is," and for the second time, a smile curled on the lips of what I admit is an otherwise unsmiling face most of the time. "Probably a million, million watts of lightning power. That's more than the combined output of all the power generators in the USA."

We sat for a while longer listening to the storm, watching mighty forces locked in mortal combat around them; raw power, concentrated fury. I looked at Miguel's son, who reminded me of Timothy.

"Those storms," I told him, "are like the air conditioners for planet Earth, taking moist air heated at the tropics and moving it fast to polar regions."

The phone interrupted the meteorological lesson. It was Liz calling long-distance from Britain. She wouldn't go into details but something was wrong. Could I return home as soon as possible?

"I've only just arrived," I groaned. "You handle it."

"Timothy is being suicidal again."

"Oh no! Look, we've been here before. Talk to him."

"What do you think I've been doing for the past three hours?"

"I can't come home before Tuesday."

"Jack, please?"

Eventually, the storm slept. But I couldn't. I thought of cruel keen winds that had blown upon my world and the disillusionment that life held for me. What had happened to the dreams? Once, I had been shaped by the prevailing idealism of the sixties, that I would be a part of a generation that would do it right this time.

But I grew weary of changing the world. In India, a late arrival on the hippie trail, I met Liz, another LSD soul with beads, blown about by life. Some years later, she had moved out of a domineering relationship with her first husband and moved in with Craig and Timothy. She was difficult. Their relationship was the curate's egg. Deep down, I knew I lacked the patience to work at the constant negotiation that marriage required.

After training as a radio officer, I would down tools and sail away for four months at a time. But my restlessness wouldn't depart so easily. Liz was a bored, troubled soul and her son from a previous relationship, Timothy, was diagnosed as schizophrenic with learning difficulties to boot. As for Liz's drugged-up older son Craig, nothing had been heard from him for a year now.

Liz blamed herself for the abuse of Timothy by a local care worker where he stayed for a while. His mum had been agreeable to his going there temporarily. But one day, the day the sky clouded over, I read that this man and his wife faced 40 charges of indecently assaulting boys under 16 in a string of incidents which took place at children's homes across the East of England. Now he had been exposed himself. When police were notified, they asked Timothy if he wanted to add to the evidence. The boy was adamant. He couldn't let him get away with it.

But the spark was short-lived. Timothy had been drained of any interest in life. When Kurt Cobain from the group Nirvana shot himself in April 1994, fans had flooded the music press with letters claiming him as the role model for a generation. America suffered a bout of copycat suicides and many young people in Britain had a similar obsession. Among them was Timothy.

Should I go home? Should I go home? No, I would wait until Tuesday. Timothy would be ok. It was just talk. No need to break the holiday for talk and one more mood swing.

The terraced house was similar to all the others; an undistinguishable terraced in an undistinguishable street in an undistinguishable London suburb. Though it was lunchtime, a pall of darkness hung visibly over the undistinguishable terrace as if it was a late gloomy winter's afternoon instead of being a sunny autumn day. I wandered around looking for signs of life.

Then, I heard sounds of sobbing from the back bedroom. I rushed down the hall to find Liz, my wife, lying on the bed, helpless with grief.

My presence in the doorway filtered through to her in the same moment that I appeared, watching in disbelief, intuitively realising what had happened. "Jack?" she said in a faltering voice. They met halfway, holding each other tightly. "It's Timothy," she cried, though I didn't need to be told. "What about Timothy?" though I didn't need to ask.

"Why didn't you get here in time?

You didn't get my message? It was phoned through to Heathrow."

"No, the plane was diverted to Manchester," I exclaimed with mounting alarm. "What message? Liz, what message?" I demanded. But I already knew.

That morning, Timothy had been late for breakfast. Liz had opened his bedroom door to find her only son had hung himself with a dressing-gown cord. Even as Liz was quietly recounting the horror of a scene she would never, never forget, I had an absurd recollection of a blue dressing gown he had bought for Timothy at Debenham's last Christmas. I had bought a murder weapon!

Then, the roar of what Liz told me began to drown out every other sound, every other thought. I was dimly aware of uncontrolled sobbing, though whether from Liz or from my own chest, I was not sure. My mind was numb, incapable of taking in an earthquake this high on the Richter scale.

Two hours later, from under the layer of numbness, raw pain began to creep along the edges of my consciousness as if an anaesthetic had worn off too quickly after a tooth had been hacked out. I pieced together what had taken place. Tim was pronounced dead at the scene by a police surgeon. Later that afternoon, I had to go to the police station. They hadn't found any suspicious circumstances. A post-mortem was being carried out and an inquest would be held in a few days.

There were people to phone; the school, Timothy's friends, Liz's sister and Steve, my half- brother. I left a message with someone who had last seen Craig, asking if he could phone urgently. I attended to it all with mechanical, heartless efficiency, hearing my own voice as a stranger announcing startling news to the uncomprehending. For two hours that evening, Liz and I sat in the unremarkable lounge, trying to get involved in an old film. There was nothing to say. What was there to say? Halfway through the night, Liz disappeared into the smart kitchen to rustle up a snack. She kept sighing deeply, hardly realising she was sighing deeply. We sat for ten minutes in the functional dining room, eyes meeting.

"This can't be true," they said a hundred times. An almost physical distress from screaming jagged nerves was rolling upon them like the tides breaking upon the shore. I wondered why I had a tight feeling in his throat, while limbs that were normally so finely tuned felt strangely numb and unyielding, as if he was a victim of a stroke, not grief.

Of all human tragedies, the greatest of all is a song unsung.

Alone with his memories lies the sleeping man. His mind, though shut down like a quiescent fire, nevertheless stores the remembrance of experiences past. Tattered memories and broken dreams, experiences framed in bright lights, experiences heavy with regret, all jostle together in the mind of the sleeping man like faces in a crowd. A hundred whispers, a conspiracy of sadness and joys stir hauntingly through the watches of the night. Heartaches, longing, despair are mixed into the same potion as laughter, lightness and joyfulness. The sleeping man drinks and drinks.

And when I wake, it is with a moment of disorientation that many experience as the flimsy shadows of sleep and confusion yield to the sturdy awareness of morning and wakefulness. "Where am I?" I wonder. "Am I at home or where?" Then, that first waking thought is transfixed and imprisoned by an impression stronger than the light pouring through the curtains. "That was no dream."

It is with a lunge to his heart that I remember what troubled me the night before. The death of a child whom he had known and held would haunt me for many years. Of that, he was sure, though the child was not his own. Timothy's Mum had just left for an ice palace of grief where loneliness is riven with cold. He would emerge soon; her sentence was only just begun.

The events of the day before now seemed a distant dream cast in unreality. It was hard to believe it was happening. I felt detached as if he were watching someone else react. Why won't the phone ring now to say it's all been a terrible mistake and my little friend is alive after all? The death of children and young people is a candle blown out though scarcely beginning to burn. Candlelight flickers into life, burns for a while and then the candle is snuffed and the light is no more. Restlessly, my thoughts follow me around that day. "Just go away," I want to say. Why was this child a song waiting to be sung with only a few notes composed? We know we are made for another song. Do only a few learn the tune that haunts us all? Though we learn to sing many tunes, the tune is only half-sung when the music fades. Perhaps unfulfilled dreams remind us of another existence rather than merely mocking us. It's all so bloody pointless! I raged and raged.

Tim's death seemed so senseless. What was the purpose of this absurd lolling about on planet Earth for a few short years? What were Tim's 15 years about? Why did it have to happen? A world where songs were cut short must be proof that God was absent without leave (or never existed except in the imagination or maybe a pleasant dream in a harsh world of nightmares). But then I pulled himself up short. Did it make any more sense to conclude that there was nothing out there that corresponds to what was inside him? The very fact that it hurt so much showed I was a thinking and feeling person. What was the source of my own humanity that cried out in the night in violent protest? Nothing seemed to make any sense.

Throughout the day, I found myself playing an old film in my mind, a film whose reels had dusted themselves off and begun to play without asking.

It was six months later, a full nine months after Timothy's suicide.

We had made a new friend. This was Liam, whom Steve had got to know in California before coming back to the UK. He put him on to us and that was ok. One day, he knocked at the door, having introduced himself over the phone the night before. I wasn't sure if Liam was a vicar-type person or a counsellor of some sort. Sounded genuine. It was odd. He seemed to know all about me, searched me and found me wanting but somehow, it didn't matter.

When he came that day, it had the ring of significance, though I didn't understand why. Liz said we must have met in a previous incarnation. She put her head round the door and called us in for lunch. Smoked salmon had been fished from somewhere and sat invitingly on bone china plates. As they ate and talked, Liz opened up, surprisingly, to this oddly compelling stranger. She spoke of a father who, after wartime service, had played out his life as a railway porter, only to be dismissed for drunkenness. She spoke of a mother in servitude to her four children, working nights to get them through college. And then she paused. "I wouldn't mind another glass of wine," she said to me. I had been listening in silence. "Coming right up," I said, uncorking a Chardonnay, playing the attentive husband. Liz sipped from a cut glass and picked up where she had left off. She spoke of Timothy. She spoke also of her other son who phoned every now and again.

Liz didn't tell him the worry now was that I had Hep C, caught from shared needles in younger days.

She said we were peas from the same pod. Once, Liz's first son Craig had been a lively and apparently healthy boy. Despite a hidden fault line running through his life, Craig was good at games, interested in fishing and plastic models of airplanes, of which he could boast several hundred. In the period when Steve and I tried hard with each other, Steve took to Craig, who had a sparkle.

Then the crevasse began to show. By the time he was 12, Craig's circle of friends knew a local drug pusher. Craig progressed from cigarettes to joints. His media-created icons were anxious to impress their devotees that they had the answers to life and everything else. On his drug-lined road to happiness, Craig began to lose interest. Motivation crept away so subtly no one knew when it went out the door. When he hit 15, he was withdrawn, knee-deep in anxiety. By his next birthday, Craig had moved from cannabis to ecstasy, joining the ranks of those who swallowed the pills of the rave culture.

"It's a dangerous short-term bid for happiness," I tried to reason with Craig when he confided in me one day. "Ecstasy damages the brain forever. You'll get chronic depression later in life. And, for goodness sake, leave heroin alone. Believe me, I know what that does to you."

But Craig wasn't going along with common sense. He felt keenly the tedium of life. Chasing the dragon helped him cope. "You don't care how much time passes," he told his mum.

Craig was no longer interested in reaching his potential. Badgering from Liz merely irritated him. Relationships with me and his little brother Timothy broke down. Hurricanes blew up without warning. One day, Craig broke Liz's glasses. It felt he had trodden on more than a pair from Specsavers. He had walked all over her. Jack said he had to go. And so he went.

Quickly, Craig's life disappeared in a haze of chemical happiness, concerned only about the next fix and living for today. Whenever Liz confronted him about his lifestyle or lack of any long-range goals, Craig staunchly maintained he could stop anytime he wanted. He would just have one more fix. Like his step-dad before him, he convinced himself that his behaviour was avant-garde and politically anarchic.

I pleaded that was a distortion of history. Craig was left in no doubt that drugs and alcohol were blanking out the pain of loneliness, artificially boosting him to feel more sociable and more alive. I recognised the mind-set. I had been there once. I grieved. This wasn't a few chic experimenters. Now, a whole generation was coming to believe that drugs or alcohol were the answer to happiness and they could control their addiction. They were wrong on both counts. But Craig hadn't listened and never stayed long in any of the jobs Liz found for him. He claimed they didn't like him there. Liz suspected this was just rationalisation. More likely, he just couldn't get to work on time.

When he was 20, Craig met Sharon. They lived for two years in a sleazy flat with the wallpaper hanging off. Liz would never forget the day Craig phoned in anguish to say that there was something wrong with the little girl he and Sharon had brought into the world. It broke her heart. But after a while, Sharon left and the child was taken into care. Craig lost his flat. He was now a dosser in Tower Hamlets but still persuaded himself that things would turn out ok. One day, he bumped into his uncle Steve. He also met a girl. They went to Manchester. She got pregnant but didn't stay on the scene for long. Craig had reached the end of the rope. Just like Timothy.

Myself and Liz were still waking up to a life where the old patterns had been rudely replaced with disorganisation. Anger, guilt and fear cascaded through us at regular intervals. In the past, despite the arguments, we were glad we had each other and would often reach out to impart, not the gift of exquisite touch we hadn't enjoyed anyway for a long, long time, but the warmth of human contact. At the beginning of Timothy's troubles and throughout all Craig's drug-taking, often we lay awake at night holding one another tightly as if to clasp life itself. If we stopped holding on, death would close up above us and we would be trapped forever in the subterranean world of the dead. Each of us was the other's lifeline to a world we glimpsed sometimes and knew was up there, a world of sunshine and of sky.

But now all that was gone. Timothy's suicide had opened up a chasm between us that went to the centre of the Earth of us but which stopped up, rather than exposed, the molten core. Nothing could have prepared us. We were frozen in time, locked away in their ice-palace, shot away from life on the warm planet where we had lived all their life, into deep space, deadly cold and from which there was no return to the world we had left behind.

The next day, Liz moved out.

After a few days, I phoned Liam to tell him. He came over.

"What with Craig, Tim's death and Liz going, life sucks," I told him. Think my voice rose with a spark of feeling as if a fire had been poked.

"During the last two months," I said, "I've been having a strange dream. It keeps recurring, especially after any deep conversations we've had."

"Tell me, Jack?" Liam enquired.

"Ok. But don't laugh. I dream that we have rooms in our house we didn't know were there. It's like...it's like there's a landing or a suite of rooms that were there all the time but remain unoccupied. The access is through a separate door, a door that I glimpse sometimes but never go through. It's one of these old wooden doors with vertical panels. One day, I'll go through and find out what lies on the other side."

"Maybe you should," said Liam. "And do something practical as well. Get a computer and surf the net. Or go and join a church or a club or something. Get yourself out and make some friends. But how's Liz? Do you expect to hear from her?"

"I know she's in bad shape too," I replied. "We should never have split up. Timothy's death was an enormous blow to our relationship though, to be fair, it hadn't been going anywhere for a while. It froze us solid so we could no longer talk to each other. But look," I pleaded, "phone her if you can. Give her a call."

Liam said he would. We talked together late into the evening about that which tears apart and that which heals, about short circuits and a run-down battery. I felt suddenly that my life might one day be recharged. If only I could shake off the guilt and anger that gripped me. If only Liz would come back. If only things could have turned out differently with Tim. If only Craig would phone. If only the appointment at the hospital wasn't what I thought it might be.

On the day her life passed its sell-by-date, Liz sat looking for hours at a twisted candlestick in her rented flat. It had been one of Timothy's experiments, an eager 12-year-old burning with curiosity to see how hot a flame should be in order to remould a metal object and turn it into another shape. The half-performed experiment had incurred her severe displeasure. The candlestick had been a gift from Jack not long after they had met. Timothy had been grounded for two weeks. Now, Liz fixed her eyes upon it with mordant interest. Slowly, delicately, she inserted a candle, then watched as it wore down and finally snuffed itself out. Liz was alone in the darkness.

"Poor candle," she said, speaking out loud to herself as she often did. And then Liz began to weep. She wept for the candle. She wept for the living candle flame of her son, prematurely extinguished. She wept for Craig. She wept for herself. "Come on," she said to herself. "Must go. Get the car out."

Liz went out of the run-down flat in the run-down street where she was now living. The clock struck 11. Scourged of any remaining peace and joy, Liz knew there was nothing left for her and nowhere else to go. She zipped up her tidal track-suit top against the chill of the night, went into the garage of the flat where she was staying and drove away in confusion. By habit, she brushed her hand against the mobile phone in her pocket, checking it was still there. Only yesterday, an odd experience happened to her in which Liz had, for an instant, pushed the button on her own landline number that recorded that she was phoned. Checking to see what the last number was and re-dialling, Liz had the oddest sensation of talking to herself. A circular internal conversation: the laugh of an empty horizon.

As if on automatic pilot, not wanting to tell herself her destination, Liz took the main A22 road down to Eastbourne and Beachy Head. Often, she and Jack had walked along its cliffs, joking about jumping. Rewind the video of her life and a young woman could be seen enjoying the delicious flattery of her first boyfriend. Once, Timothy had crept along its chalky banks and an anxious mum had restrained him. "Don't go too near, Tim. Just look from a safe distance." Now Timothy had gone too close to the edge, jumping a jump of no--return into...into what? What lay beyond death?

Once, Liz lived in a green world bathed by golden sunshine. In the unquiet moments of tossing night, she would hear Mum and Dad call to her as they always used to. Her mother was a warm, busy, chapel-going sainted lady. Her dad was a farmer who loved Liz but disguised it heavily amidst a strict regime. As a girl, she could always be found by the lake near their home in the Welsh mountains. Then her mum passed away and death dried up the lake and exhausted the sun.

Within the halls of her memory, Liz heard the stable door bang as it had done again and again on a windy Welsh night. The wind of Timothy's death hunted through her. Was that what her life had been? A life where a stable door bangs and the horses were restless and the keen wind hunted through every crack?

As she gripped the steering wheel, she thought of an odyssey she had made when the only man she had really loved amongst her college conquests married someone his mother disapproved of less than she did of her. Liz had simply not been up to the mark to be a fit daughter-in-law for such a person. On the wedding day, the stable door shut, Liz set off on a pilgrimage to an unknown destination. She had been unsure of her destination then. For two years, Liz groped for a natural way to live, going back through the layers of modern living, mass production, mass consumption and mechanistic science, hungry for a sense of meaning and belonging.

What an odyssey that had been. Liz visited new-age California, studied with Indian holy men, sought healing from native American shamans, indulged in trance dancing to African drums and had visited sacred Celtic sites. She had learned Tantric lovemaking, the power of silence and celebrated the return of the goddess. In India, she met Jack, both late arrivals on the hippie trail in the mid-1970s.

The odyssey continued. On a Midsummer day at Stonehenge, she had danced with the Druids. Even in flat-earth suburbia, the search for Eden was relentless. She remembered what Liam had written in an article she read.

"The mansion of eternity must always be occupied with something; the shelves of the supermarket are never empty", adding something else that was illuminated in her memory like an object lit up by the headlights of her car. "The paradox in this circular spirituality these days is that we cry out for meaning. But all we find is ourselves, the reflection of our own face staring back at us."

Liz now wondered if everything had been to serve her, making the gods work for you, an extended conversation with herself. As the car took her to its un-programmed destination, it struck her that she was once again talking out loud to herself, a habit she had acquired when Jack had been away for four months at a stretch. But it really went further back, to the time when she lay awake at nights listening to the stable door banging and the keen wind hunting through every crack.

In the 70s had come, for a brief moment, the opening of the stable door to find that the great love of her life was tantalisingly available to her. Their rendezvous on Beachy Head, as the wind hunted round them, resulted in the conception of Timothy. Or so she imagined in a fond moment. Then the door banged shut once more. She could see so much of herself in Timothy, even the features of her face. As Timothy became interested in the toys of Star Wars, Liz had been fascinated with the scene where Luke Skywalker sees Darth Vader and, in the mask, comes face to face with his own reflection. "Timothy will never see the Prequel," she said, though alone in the car.

Liz suddenly saw through the emptiness of the mood she had willingly embraced, a spirituality rising and falling into itself, consumer religion, whose purpose (it was said) is to help the soul understand its own inner workings. Yet another conversation interminable and internal. That's what her life had been then. No one there.

Jack had never understood but while she had genuinely loved him, he had been too morose for her. She felt someone had signed away her life. Jack had never been good in bed. She had often wondered whether sex was the new religion, the quest for experience of some other world, yearning for someone outside ourselves to encounter, to take us over, the drive towards hell, the drive towards heaven. Was that why sex had been boring, Liz dimly wondered? If it was only a way of finding wholeness and fulfilment, maybe sex was yet one more internal conversation.

As she turned off the main A22 road, Liz gripped the steering wheel. For a flickering moment she thought she saw a cigar-shaped object hover overhead. With lambent curiosity, eyes straining, she watched, fascinated. "Come back!" she called out as the cigar-shaped object vanished into the perpetual night that now occupied her. Dramatic words from another sci-fi blockbuster Timothy enjoyed came back to her. He had walked round the house declaring, "the question of whether we are alone in the universe has finally been settled".

Liz turned towards Beachy Head. The night was chilly.

"Why is there such an indifference to our fate? Is there anyone out there?" she called out, just as when a little girl heard the stable door banging in the night. The 50 years since the Roswell incident had stamped the second half of the 20th century with the idea of a world being visited. A society that couldn't stand living in a lonely universe scanned the skies anxiously. So far, all that had been found was a reflection of ourselves, seeing what we wanted to see. Nothing and no one there.

Liz parked, then wandered along the cliff area in the silence of the night. Was she going to end it all? She didn't know. If she was, this was the best place, where Timothy had been conceived and where mother and son had returned on those long months when Jack was away. "Don't go too near the edge," she had said to him on many occasions. But he had. And so this was the best place.

Across the cliff top, she walked for a while, picking her way along the path by the light of a low moon that hung over the sea. She paused occasionally to shoot her voice over the water that surged against the rocks far below. Seagulls flew around with angry moans. By now, it was three in the morning. Liz couldn't bear the thought of another night coming on. The void calling beneath her was something she would fall into, never to rise again.

Then Liz had an urge to pray. After her childhood faith had evaporated into college intellectualism, a process confirmed by her journeys overseas, any idea of prayer had the process of meditation, realising the godhood of self, the control of the life-breath. In her present mood, suddenly that seemed to be yet another conversation with herself. She tried again, placing a call in the old, old way of communicating that she hadn't tried for a long, long time. "God, if you're there," she cried out in misery, "show yourself to me. Is anyone there?"

Silence. Nothing. No one. That was it then. For three or four minutes, Liz stood, suspended on the edge of the abyss. She could not turn herself back to the solid cliff behind and prepared to take a step into the ultimate experience of nothingness. And then a coincidence. A ridiculous, unsettling conjunction; two separate points of the universe colliding that should never have come together.

Chapter Eleven:

Redemption's Happy Hour

As Liz took a step into the chasm of sea and darkness beneath, just then, the phone rang. What on earth? Here? Of course, it was the mobile phone still in her coat pocket. As if wandering disconsolately along the cliff at Beachy Head in the little hours was sufficiently unreal, this was surreal. "Go on, answer it," she said out loud. Instinct took hold as the curiosity of the self she had been about to extinguish rose from the abyss. The indivisible blackness of sea and sky suddenly looked less intense.

"Hello," she said. She couldn't believe it. Liam, of all people? Here on the phone? Now? This time of night! It had to be the oddest thing that had ever happened.

"Liz, I had the strangest and strongest impulse to phone you. I know how late it is. And you will tell me to back off and go to bed. But something has made me call. Tell me you're ok."

Liz took a deep breath and couldn't resist smiling at the situation. Maybe all her experience did not have to be a long extended conversation with oneself. Perhaps there was someone out there able to break in upon us. What should she say?

"Yes, I'm all right." Even as she said these words, she felt herself struggle back over the cliff to find a foothold on life once more. "Look, thanks for phoning. I'll go back now," (though she didn't say where she was). "Come and talk to me soon," she added, almost as an afterthought. Liz thought she saw a crack in the sky. And she sat there for an hour until pale flecks of morning began to line the eastern sky. A new day.

Liam and Liz met quite often after that. Once a week would see them in Starbucks talking about faith and framework – and whether the latter was helpful for the former. Liam said it was the lack of a framework that made it hard for end-of-millennium people to find the voice of faith and put their world together. They discussed whether there is something beyond. Liz wasn't up for much of it. She couldn't deny that, at a level deeper than the life of the mind, she had responded –or not as the case, maybe, but to life in a certain way.

"I don't think there's anything there that comes to us from outside," she said emphatically, "It's all what comes to us from within. We create our own solutions, our own redemption."

"So, tell me what led up to that night on Beachy Head?" Liam probed gently.

Liz fell silent. After a while and a second Latté, she told him what was going on before that. Her bid for an air of easy-going self-composure began to crumple.

"You're right," she admitted. "I needed help from outside that wild night. All the self-talk pick-me-ups were suddenly hollow. But don't you need proof? You can't believe anything."

"You've got to take a leap to be sure," said Liam. "But unlike you that night, it wouldn't be a leap into the unknown, or more obviously, into the nothingness of certain death. If it's

Christian faith we're talking, it makes complete sense, but at some point, you have to jump."

"You seem very sure of all this," said Liz. "I suppose that's what comes of training to be a vicar. You should go and convert my brother-in-law Steve," she said. "They're back in the UK now. Silicon Valley, where he worked until recently, is a frenetic place. Unless you bring your full self into work with you, you should go find somewhere else to be."

"I expect you know I've met him?" said Liam.

"Yes, I heard," Liz nodded. "It must be tough to keep moving at the required pace. Attentional overload is what they call it. The non-stop emails, texts, messages, meetings - just creates a hill of stress. It's like you're expecting the alarm to go off every minute."

"That's for sure," agreed Liam. "You get to work and suddenly its lunchtime. And then you remember, you haven't even had breakfast!"

"But look, I am listening," Liz said. "Maybe one of these days I'll take the leap of faith. "Think he's left for good that lady he was friendly with?" Liz asked, her tone heavy with euphemism.

"Hope so," said Liam. "Beth has powerful allure for him. Steve was the moth drawn to light."

"Hope you can meet and chat sometime soon," Liz said. "Think he's in denial about all that."

They parted shortly afterwards, Liz returning to her temporary accommodation. She wasn't sure if she and Jack would get back. She said she got lonely sometimes but now had a Pentium!

"Well, that wasn't an easy day!" remarked Katie as they drove home from the funeral.

"Certainly wasn't," agreed Bill. "Uncle Len was a father to me and a Granddad to you. He was a good man."

"Very poignant we couldn't see him before he died," Katie said. "This is so hard on people."

"Yes, it is," Bill agreed. "Thought Liam did a good job taking the graveside service but it rubs it in that we couldn't get more than a dozen there and those that did needed to stand away from each other. It highlighted the distress of these days. We're not made to stand apart and keep our distance."

"It's all so weird, Dad," Katie said, glancing as she drove at the embattled face Bill showed. "Stay indoors, stay away, stay separate but we all came together somehow."

"What we have got is technology," Bill observed. "A hundred years ago, we didn't have any of this magic in the last global pandemic. With AIDS, we didn't have anything on this scale."

"Home learning is happening in theory," remarked Katie. "I would say just over half of our pupils' parents are engaged with their children's doing lessons online."

"It's all going to increase the divides teachers like you have been working to close for some time," said Bill, watching the trees and lampposts merging.

"That's true," agreed Katie. "Teachers from the most deprived schools report a much lower parental engagement than those from the least deprived schools. The shift to remote learning during lockdown has made the implications of children and young people's unequal access to IT equipment and connection even more stark. We have to help these children to catch up. Some of our children who already face the greatest challenges have suffered the worst impact to their learning during the lockdown. The digital divide is largely to blame."

"Covid-19 has changed our older students' expectations of what the university experience will be," she added. "They fear the social aspect will be almost non-existent. Covid changed the future. All that freedom of adulthood! They'll be stuck at home doing lectures online."

"Sure," agreed Bill. "You enjoyed university. It was a good time for you."

"The sister of my friend Maddie is still hoping to go to University in September," remarked Katie as they turned off the motorway.

"But you know, Dad, I had been really looking forward to joining societies and clubs like hockey, but for this generation, how can a Zoom call give you that experience?" I personally find face-to-face learning much more useful than online teaching," she said. "But the world is changing fast and young people will just have to get on and deal with whatever may happen."

"Find love online?" asked Bill, watching for clues in Katie's expression. She smiled.

"We had a Zoom date last night," Katie said. "That was different! Neither Robert nor I wanted to rush into another relationship, but it feels good."

"How do you do a Zoom date online, for goodness sake?" Bill asked. "Wondered why you wanted the meal in your room!"

"Dad, it was fun. Candlelit dinner, a glass or three – all very romantic."

"Very different from when you were a baby at the time of AIDs when your Mum died and we were just getting on to Internet Relay Chat," Bill said, instantly wishing he hadn't.

Katie went quiet. They drove the rest of the way in silence as Bill remembered what Jack, his school-boy partner in crime, had told him over a drink one night years ago.

It was still fast for 1999. One morning, Jack Bright purchased his first Pentium. It ran at 333 MHz and came complete with a modem and Internet access to the mysterious world of cyberspace.

Quickly, he began to be hooked on email and USENET newsgroups. But despite these services that seemed impossibly futuristic to anyone only ten years before, Jack Bright yearned for something more. If only he could have a real conversation with someone rather than a game of phone tag; 'first my turn, then yours'.

Cyberspace was a new world. Often, Jack wondered where it actually was. Using your mouse, you could buy anything from Viagra to Venetian blinds. You could enter a bookshop and browse through a global selection of four million titles. Given the right equipment, you could get into web TV or trade stocks and shares on the Net. Virtual reality appealed to him. It was a growth industry everywhere. Jack began to feel more at home in cyberspace than the real world, whatever that was. He spent hours walking into virtual art galleries, being shown round the White House or watching the world go by through a camera in New York. And there was porn too, complete with 360-degree imaging of bodies, voyeurs from any direction. Jack savoured it, though only temporarily. It all seemed hollow to him now.

One day, he discovered Internet Relay Chat. "Hmm," thought Jack as he sat in front of the manual. He worked out how to adjust configuration and settings, got online, and by trial and error, went through the steps. Now he was ready to go.

In the next few days, Jack familiarised himself with the current lingo. He would need user ID by which he would be known. Every line of text he would send to the network would be prefixed by this nickname. He chose a boyhood hero, a role he had loved to play. Alexander the Great. Jack typed in "/nick Great Alex".

Up came a welcome message on the server. "Welcome to the Internet Relay network." He entered a command to find out which channels had at least ten people on them. Chat lines were operating 24 hours a day in a world that never slept.

Within a month, Jack was hooked. He was back at the graduation ball. People from all over the world stood around in groups. Anytime he wanted, he could join in their conversations or eavesdrop for a while, walk from group to group and even invite someone into a separate room to have a private chat. That was how he met 'Jude'.

It was a chance encounter. And their first private channel did not last longer than three minutes before there was a 'G ' for gone next to her nickname. But the following week, there was an 'H'. Jude was back.

Jude: Hi. It's me.

Great Alex: Hello again.

Jude: ASL, right?

Great Alex: Fine by me. Age is 40-50; sex, yes please and I'm male. Location- somewhere south of London.

Jude: Our profiles are similar. My age is 40-50; sex, not yet and by the way, I'm female. Location? somewhere to the north of you but not that much.

That was how it started. At first, chat sessions averaged once a fortnight. They notched it up to once a week and then hardly a day would go by without some message from the mysterious 'Jude'. For some time, Jack was happy to abide by the rules. Jude could be anybody. A married woman having a fling? His neighbour even? Who knows? That was the adventure of the cyber community.

Jack had begun by using a log file to save all his IRC sessions. But there was such drivel. He remembered CB radio in his teenage days. All this hi-tech didn't mean that human beings suddenly had profound things to say to each other. So why did he think his chat correspondence with the mysterious Jude produced gems that were worth keeping? Jack told himself off for keeping love letters as if he was playing the role of all lovers throughout history. But he couldn't bring himself to erase the files.

Jude: Hi. It's me again.

Great Alex: You hung up the other day before I could ask you something.

Jude: Ask me what?

Great Alex: Hey Jude, why Jude?

Jude: No big secret. The Beatles are still my favourite.

Great Alex: Mine too! 'Yesterday, all my troubles seem so far away!'

Jude: We seem to have a few things in common.

A phone rang in suburbia.

"Dad?" went a sallow voice.

"Craig? Craig!" said Jack in a groggy voice. It was the first time for years that Craig had called him that. Memories of a shy little boy instantly stood to attention. "Craig, where are you?"

"Can you come?"

"What time is it?" asked Jack.

"About 2 am I think," said the scared voice on the other end of the phone. "Look, I'm at Casualty. There's a problem. I need help."

"I'll be right there," said Jack and quickly dressed.

At Casualty, he pieced together what had happened. Craig had been sleeping round a mate's house for the past three nights. They had run short of hash. His mate had approached the dealer for more dope. He had given him 20 pounds but then realised, too late, that he hadn't collected the change. The dealer was known to turn quickly and the lads quaked. Wanting to act tough and unafraid, Craig said he'd sort it, though inside he was petrified. The pusher was dealing with someone else when Craig showed up demanding his change. Things quickly got out of hand. Craig got beaten up with a cricket bat. The pusher had been arrested for assault though Craig didn't know how long he would be locked up.

Jack sat looking around him as they waited for Craig to be seen to and for the police to take a statement. It was 2.45 in the morning. One man sat with his head in his lap, holding a towel to his eyes. "It was meant to make you mad!" erupted a loud voice in the corner.

A fight had developed outside a nightclub. The bouncer intervened and in the scuffle, pushed them through a shop window. Across hospitalised rows of red seats, both parties now glared at each other. It struck Jack as a little picture of hell, an advance warning of a day of reckoning. "What a mess," he thought. "People blowing it and lashing out. They're trapped," he thought. "Guess I'm trapped, trapped in my bleak, sad solitary existence."

Craig spoke about the change that had been coming over him, that he was beginning to put distance between him and King H.

"I thought heroin was a dependable friend. It relieved the pain just as the effect of the last dose began to wear off."

"Craig, maybe you've got to speak it out and say ' I don't need this anymore...you're no friend of mine!"

They chatted for a while, watching hurting people meander through the reception area. Occasionally, a nurse walked briskly through from one end to another. In the middle of the night, everyone and everything was daubed with grim colours.

"Where did you and Mum meet?" asked Craig curiously.

"In India," Jack replied. But that was as far as he got. Just then, Craig went to make a statement. Jack sat looking at the tear-stained lives and anger that sicked up all over the place. The record in Casualty that night stirred him deeply. "We definitely pay," thought Jack, "just like someone's going to pay for that shop window."

Craig was there for ages, being interviewed and being stitched up. Jack fell into as sound a sleep as a hard chair in Casualty would allow, dreaming of India and the last time he and Liz had visited there together. Maybe they would go again. Please, God!

India. A bewildering human drama where the scenes were changing incessantly and disturbingly. Scenes of beauty and ugliness, poverty and wealth, peacefulness and noise, luxury and squalor alternated rapidly and with a contrast that was profoundly unsettling. Jack Bright and Liz knew that they would be as affected by the encounter as any amongst the caravan of western travellers before them.

A 20-hour journey by train brought them to Varanasi Junction. They had arrived at the ancient capital of Hindu faith and learning. Once in a lifetime, Hindus visited old Benares to wash away their sins. Jack looked nostalgically at the familiar sights.

"It was Mark Twain who said 'Benares is older than history, older than tradition, older even than legend and looks twice as old as all of them put together'," he remarked to Liz. "To die here is to be most favourably placed to ensure the best possible rebirth."

After checking into a low-budget hotel, they sought the services of a rickshaw guide. They could have made it around by foot but Jack said it would be good for a first-time visit. A guide would stop them being pestered by beggars and fake Sadhus after their money. And so, in the twilight world of early evening, they found themselves carted around a mysterious world populated by dope fiends, money lenders, holy men and roadside barbers. Purveyors in the silk emporium followed the traditions of centuries. When a royal prince Siddartha, the Buddha had prized the silks of Benares. If Jack and Liz were lost amidst the countless bazaars and stalls, they needn't have worried, the rickshaw guide explained. Following a sacred cow or a funeral procession would always return them to familiar landmarks.

The wind of the night stirred fretfully against the windows of the hotel and the travellers had arranged to be woken an hour before dawn. Their guide was waiting. He pulled them in silence through winding alleys dominated by mountains of incense, fruit and vegetables. The skyline was dominated by domes, towers, minarets and hundreds of temples dedicated to Shiva, presiding deity of old Benares.

Jack and Liz were drawn to an unforgettable kaleidoscope of temple priests, pyres of smouldering people and old ruined temples sliding into a river. They had arrived at the Ganges. Hindu pilgrims crowded on to the Ghats, stepped embankments along the riverbank, and prepared for a ritual bath and the ceremony of Puja in praise of the rising sun. Thousands stood, waiting for priests to summon the dawn. Then came the huge redness of the rising sun; with it, a broken silence. Ghats draped in the mistiness of early morning suddenly woke to life. The faithful flocked into the river to wash clothes along with their sins.

Pyres were being lit for the first cremations of the day. The rickshaw guide explained that ghats were different; one had a shrine to the goddess of smallpox, another was used for cremating the bodies of outcasts, one was dedicated to ascetics and yet another, the Hanuman Ghat, was the scene of worship to the monkey god. The furthest embankment was the first of five special Ghats that pilgrims must bathe in during the course of a single day in order to fulfil a complete purification ritual. By the riverbank, sick people lay on filthy rags or mats of rattan, waiting to die. As the sun began to build in intensity, Jack and Liz were glad to pause under a tree that offered shade. They reached the market. A dozen butcher's stalls were killing animals right there on the street. Car horns were blown obsessionally.

Jack pointed out where Brahman priests used to observe the Asva Medha, the most important sacrifice in old Hinduism. It took a whole year commencing with ritual sacrifice of 609 horses in exactly the right order. But get it right and performing the Asva Medha gave unlimited saving power. Jack knew of the old priestly literature, the Brahmanas. 'This is the atonement for everything, the remedy for everything'," he intoned. "'He who performs the Asva Medha, redeems all sin. Whosoever performs the Asva Medha sacrifice, obtains all his desires, and attains all attainments.'"

"India's millions," Liz observed, "are told that the problem with the human race has been that we are trapped; trapped on an endless round of birth and rebirth- Samsara, the constant flow of the human soul from one form of life to another. What we need is Moksha, freedom, so we can be released from the wheel of life to which we are hopelessly bound."

As if in harmony with this statement, bicycle wheels were glinting in the sun. Occasionally, their riders stopped to get off. Was it possible to get off the cycle and find freedom? You've got to build up enough karma, Jack said. But how do you ever know if there is enough in your personal account? The consequences of actions follow you about forever like chains on a condemned man. Is forgiveness possible, real forgiveness that clears away the past? It was a question that hung in the air.

It was early evening in early summer of the last year before the twentieth century took its farewell. Liam moved briskly along the top of the circular mound that curved across the old Neolithic hill fort of Cissbury Ring on the chalk hills of the English South Downs. Colour in the green-grey sky was receding, leaving him alone underneath fading light. He came here sometimes to commune with his father. But he was not alone. A man with jet black hair and a black heavy-knit Sherpa fleece was walking briskly along the top of the mound from the opposite direction, his legs moving easily beneath a stocky body, his emotions bleeding from soul-emptiness. Eyes locked with simultaneous recognition. They surveyed each other with an approving air, then spoke out their greeting.

Bill Trimble's voice sounded. "Here you are! Ok?"

"I'm ok. Good to see you Bill!" said Liam.

Bill had phoned earlier that day. They had arranged to meet up when it transpired that he was lecturing in astronomy in Brighton at the university that week and Bill had a couple of hours between sessions. They hadn't spoken since Liam had visited San Francisco.

They talked for a while about family and friends.

"But tell me. Do they take you seriously?" Bill asked, in a flush of genuine curiosity despite himself. There was something enigmatic about his eyes, brimming with friendliness but on a closer view, not wanting to disclose his inner turmoil.

"I think they're starting to," Liam replied. "People are genuinely searching, I think. I've seen enough on my journey to know that spirituality is the buzz of our times. It's not 'do you believe', like it was in our younger days. It's 'what do you believe!' Some sort of faith is everywhere."

Aware that he did not have long, there came upon Bill an impulse to reveal his inner thoughts to this man. They stood looking out over soft green downs. Bill was in pensive mood. From his fleece pocket, he withdrew a newspaper.

"Have you seen this?"

The headline for the 12th March in that year of 1998 proclaimed that asteroid XF11 was on collision course with Earth. October 2028 was the target.

"These are interesting times we live in," said Liam. "There's almost a sense of history building to a conclusion."

"It gets to me," Bill said suddenly, surveying the evening. "If I was to go in for religion, I wouldn't side with those who convey an easy familiarity with the cosmos. I want to stand awe-struck before everything that is beautiful. I want to cease living in a drab, functional world drained of astonishment. Where's the magic in the mundane?" As he said this, he looked surprised that he could even admit thoughts like this, let alone articulate them. But something about Liam drew him out.

"If only religion didn't involve giving power away to an organisation," he continued. "If it was about connecting to the divine through the beauty of nature, or unconditional love for human beings, I'd be in. Any ideal is always spoilt."

Liam stopped and looked earnestly at him.

"But it's equally messy," he said, "when it comes to working out any ideal, like marriage for instance. It's inevitable that wherever you get people doing something in community together, not just indulging an individual whim, there will be an institutional, organised aspect to things which can then go wrong. But you're right, of course," he added. "The church has struggled with its humanity like we all do individually."

Bill paused to pick the bud off a tree that hung limply beside the footpath. Beneath them, the sea glistened. There was no stopping the overflow of the dam.

"I'm tired of a sardonic rationalism and the materialism that's blighted my life," he said despairingly. "I'm tired of the props being the centre of the stage. There has to be more."

They slowly walked down the hillside.

"We all have," said Liam slowly, "a hunger to experience a reality greater than what we could touch and see. We built this universe boxed in by the horizons of what we could prove with our tiny mind, what we could calculate, what we could buy. But we couldn't live in such a confined prison. We needed to depose arrogant rationalism, to rediscover a spiritual dimension and make the world an enchanted place once again."

Bill reflected on this for a moment. He felt himself cracking and crumbling. "I am curious about the spirit zone in the self-development courses I have attended in Esalen," he said. "Wasn't like the summer of love in 67 in San Francisco," he added. "I was too young for that one but you still got marijuana, mescalen and LSD taken in large quantities. Drug-induced mysticism or psychedelics as agents for personal and social change! On arrival for my course, the guests were handed a drink of beetroot and orange. The food was light and healthy and you should have seen the bedrooms!"

"What about them?" Liam asked curiously.

"They came complete with a frankincense pillow spray to encourage relaxation and a bedside booklet to suggest how you could wind down, assuming you were still stressed after a late evening reflexology session in the health club or a head and neck massage for those who needed it. It's all about creating karma, I think, but it's got a good spiritual feel to it. "Mind you, we need something to tell us how to take a deep breath and focus on priorities."

Liam looked at his friend inquiringly.

"Look around," he said. "At this end of millennium moment, there's a vast range of products available - health foods, alternative medicine, altered states of consciousness, positive thinking, smudging, self-help courses to help maximise your human potential. It's spiritual thirst. The ordinary stuff doesn't work anymore. We need more and more, like sailors who drank salt water and died with a raging thirst. What we really need is fresh water."

"I've been doing a lot of thinking recently," said Bill gesticulating at the darkening night sky above them, "what with Ali's being seriously ill with Aids. Ok, I'm a person, I hurt. But is there any echo? Does the universe respond to my cry to count, to be conscious, to be loved and valued? Or is all our humanity met with a cruel mocking laugh, like…. like the laugh of an empty horizon?"

"How can the spirit keep intact in a place where everything is evaporated as the dew of morning?" said Liam. "And what is it about us that we even ask such questions?" he added. "You, me, those people over there," he said, indicating a couple strolling up the hill, "we're all born with a gap. There's a hole. It needs explaining. Even more, it needs filling."

"You know what my lecture is about?" Bill asked Liam rhetorically. "The structure of the universe has been a perennial quest over two and a half thousand years or more. In the past century, a deeper quest has been the concern of theoretical physicists. How is everything connected? With the addition of the Higgs field, the fundamental forces are fairly well known, but how they fit together is another matter. What is the nature of reality?"

"You know, Bill," Liam said, "we hold our arguments about the greatest question of all; we can bat them back and forward as in that Ideas Group you came to in San Francisco that time.

But that gap you speak of is frighteningly real. Is there an anything out there that corresponds to what's in here? Does the cosmos give any personal meaning to our lives?

"As the dimensions of the cosmos have exploded into unimaginative scale, human insignificance seems smaller and smaller. Yet, there is a huge gap. Our personal lives protest hugely against being written off. The gap is between the objective laws of physics and the everyday subjective experience that yearns for significance. For me, that takes us straight to the existence of God."

"How do you get to that from the question of our own need to count?" asked Bill curiously.

"So, here's the thing," said Liam as they returned to the car park below Cissbury Ring. "What ultimate realities are suggested by the drive to feel we are significant, that we count? How does the universe generate human participants who not only are conscious and self-aware but have an imperative towards high worth? Or has an impersonal universe given rise to this fundamental way we are wired up? A personal God is the most satisfactory explanation of valuable personhood. We can object all we want but we only have to look within to know we need to be of value as people. What's that based on?"

Bill nodded occasionally under these blows to his old, crumbling mindset. When his clutch was engaged, he could drive through intellectual arguments with the best of them. But he could no longer deny that he was born with a gap. By now, they were strolling down the long slope that leads to the car park. An approaching couple talked together with honeyed voices and furtive expressions on their faces. Bill thought of Beth and knew he loved her.

"I've come to this spot because this is where I used to wander as a boy when I wanted to think things over. I came here many times after Jerusalem. Why, I wonder, do we create special places, full of mystery?" he added intently.

Liam stared at him, lingering over the incalculable outcome of that fateful day. Liam still had no idea who he was. Now wasn't the time.

"Where are you staying?" Liam asked, deflecting the blow to his ancient wound.

"The Grand Hotel," said Bill. "That's where the IRA tried to blow up the entire British cabinet in 1984. It's rebuilt now, of course. Look," he added, "when I return to the UK, let's meet."

They said their farewells and Bill returned to the conference and flew back to America.

Two days later, Bill sat looking at the fog that had once again enveloped San Francisco. He imagined himself at home in the restless sea, forever in turmoil, forever yearning upwards. Strong winds were driving the water. A dark grey restlessness hung over him like a cloud through which little penetration by the sun was possible. He remembered the many times when he had longed for a shaft of warmth and light to dissipate his cold joyless life.

"Guilt is the heavy burden I must carry round with me. I'm paying," Bill had said to Liam. "And others pay for me. You won't find the answer to that at the bottom of a bottle."

"Very true," Liam had said. "Where will you find the answer?"

"We choose," said Bill, turning heavy eyes upon Bill and holding him in his stare. "And we live with the consequences forever!"

"No, we don't," said Liam. "There's a way out. It's a road called forgiveness. To be forgiven and to forgive breaks the chains as nothing else can."

Liam had related an old story. Bill knew of it. It was of two brothers. The youngest brother pleaded with their father to give him his inheritance now, without waiting around until the old man died. With a heavy heart, the father agreed to it and watched as his son trod the pathway to fame, fortune and fast living. It didn't work out. Aiming high, the youngest son spent and spent until he sunk low because he had spent everything. He sunk so low that he became a feeder of pigs, which was as low as you could get in those days. One day, he came to his senses. What on earth was he was doing there? "I will arise," he said to himself, "and go to my father." Which he did. And the warmth of the welcome took his breath away and was spoken of for centuries.

It was August 1999

Great Alex: Did you see the sunset tonight?

Jude: The evening was ablaze. Someone soaked the sky in paraffin and lit it

Great Alex: I knew a lady once who could set the sky alight

Jude: Now that's a fine thing to say to me.

Great Alex: I really hope this isn't a step too far. I think I'm falling in love

Jude: I feel that too. Perhaps we should meet and feel the vibes between us

Great Alex: Speaking of the future, are you going to the eclipse?

Jude: Yes, I'm going with some friends. Are you?

Great Alex: Sure. When I was a boy, I read that the last great eclipse of the century could be seen from Britain. I made up my mind there and then I'd see it.

Jude: Alex, or whatever your name is, let's not play anymore.

Great Alex: You need to explain that

JudeWe've been online friends now for ages. Let's meet.

Great Alex: I was hoping you'd say that

With mutual trepidation, it was agreed. And so were a rendezvous point and means by which they could spot one another amidst the spectators. Great Alex would wear a red striped shirt, a mauve jacket and would be sporting a small black holdall. Jude would wear a cream coloured top and have a dahlia tied to her handbag.

They had feared Cornwall would sink under the weight of several million visitors. Amongst the invaders were druids, New

Agers plus other assorted pagans come to commune with the earth and heaven, with myth and with mystery. Like tourists making a beeline for a continental beach, sacred sites and monuments that dotted the Cornish firmament were ideal for the nature-based spirituality of modern paganism. The eclipse was a great time for giving birth.

Amongst the crowds come to see a once-in-a-lifetime nature spectacular, Jack looked out for someone who might answer to Jude's description. In the heaving sea, there was little hope of finding a stranger. Waiting for the moment when the sun would be blotted out, Jack mused why it was that men in a second marriage often ended up going for a wife-look-alike. He waited with anticipation for the eclipse and for Jude. As the tension of the crowd began to solidify, he caught the mesmerising event unfolding before him. Most of Cornwall was draped in rain cloud. But where they were, a gap suddenly appeared.

Yesterday, the warmth of an August sun had filled the morning and Jack felt the power of an energy machine so vast it defied comparison with anything else in the solar system. Now, the moon arose to stand directly in the way, turning day into night. Through special glasses, he and thousands more continued to watch as the sun and moon wrestled for control of the day. Flames licked round the side of the moon.

Two minutes passed before the issue was no longer in doubt and the sun reappeared in the blazing glory of a raging, unending, nuclear conflagration. Once again, it was converting ferocious energy to light and heat to radiate out across the solar system.

"Who lit the fire at the centre of the sun?" Jack pondered. And it seemed to him that the curtain had fallen on the old century but that the sun had re-appeared and there was hope.

But nowhere was there any sign of anyone who might be Jude. Then he saw Liz. Jack stood mesmerised, unable to break free from the magnetic earth. His ex-partner was wearing the same top and jacket and had the same bag as Jude was supposed to have. Liz was Jude. Jude was Liz! The moon that was Liz had just obliterated the sun that Jude represented for him. Jude was now eclipsed forever. For a while, they hugged without words. Then words began to flow, expressions of thoughts that should have been uttered long before, a river of words and a disclosure of emotions that continued as they drove back to the family home. Liz was stirred by the transformation of an uncommunicative man into someone who seemed to actually enjoy articulating his inner mind.

That was how Alex and Jude met up again as Jack and Liz. A month later found them talking and walking for an evening and a long night along the Thames embankment and streets of London that were beginning to empty. It was warm enough to allow a conversation that was unremitting, full of lost tenderness. Both were surprised how easy it was to make the transition from cyberspace to reality. Both wondered if such a jump was itself artificial.

As they passed a restaurant boat moored on the Thames, Jack said, "Look, in December I've got a reunion with Steve and Bill Trimble, an old friend from school. Amanda is coming. Will you come as my surprise date?"

"Yes, sure," said Liz. "Why not? Let's do it. How are Steve and Amanda, by the way?"

As the world was slowly enveloped in darkness, the city slipped into a different phase of life. Most formal work in the office block world was winding down. Office blocks pierced the sky and buildings of all kinds were silhouetted against the gathering night. But even as the lights were coming on, the city was coming alive with a beat and an excitement that was palpable. Out there in the inky world were restaurants and wine bars, cinema complexes, throbbing nightclubs and shops that stayed open till late.

"I love city life," thought Steve contentedly. "Give me the shops, the people and the entertainment you get in the city. There's a vibrancy here you just can't beat."

As a student, he had decided the only way he could have the life he aspired to was to stay in the city but to try to live more cheaply. That was another tension with Mandy. Despite working in both San Francisco and now London, she hated the city.

"Dirty, sprawling urban monsters that gobble up people and countryside," she called them. Their daughter Jane had sung that song too once. "Cities oppress humanity, overshadowing the rustic simplicity of life with concrete mistakes!"

The lift stopped and out popped Jane. They had arranged to meet up and eat out together that night. For a few minutes, they stood there, trying unsuccessfully to see stars behind the neon glare of night.

"Through a telescope," said Jane, "I once saw Hercules, city of 100,000 stars."

Steve looked at Jane, a growing respect forming for his daughter. Jane already seemed perfectly at home in the BBC, exuding the kind of breezy confidence he associated with his peers in business or the lawyers Amanda rubbed shoulders with. The ups and downs of home life didn't seem to have left her too scarred.

Father and daughter went into Starbucks and ordered coffee.

"I think you'll be good at children's TV, actually," he said proudly. "You'll relate well to slightly older kids who, like you at that age, enjoy bright colours and pop music. Even as a child, you had a maddening mix of innocence and naughtiness."

"Naughtiness?!" Jane exclaimed. "Dad, you haven't exactly been My Good Boy! Our family life hasn't been blissful."

"I've had to learn the hard way that happiness was learning when to go home," remarked her father, biting his lip.

"Are you still working all the hours?" Jane enquired.

"It's easier now," sighed Steve. "Before I had the business, I worked for companies that demanded complete commitment from staff. It initiates you into a long-hours culture. You're drained of time or energy to be with your family or pursue your interests. There's not much time for anything else there."

"How's Uncle Jack?" she said suddenly. "I thought I saw him the other day."

"He's trying to patch things up with Liz after all that's happened."

"Look, Dad," Jane said, slowly increasing pressure on his arm, "since we're talking reconciliation, contact brother Ben. He needs you. Don't believe his air of 'I'm all right'. "

"Will do," Steve replied. "Mind you, I reckon I've got some accounting to do with the past. Everyone's gotta to go home and pay their dues. It's about time I went and paid mine."

"You mean with Mum?" Jane asked.

"No, much further back than that," her Dad replied. "It's what took place when I was a boy."

Israel, May 1971. It was the last day of the school trip.

In Jerusalem, the six-day war had been a half of that as Israeli paratroops encircled East Jerusalem and the old city. By the end of June '67, the Israeli Government declared the reunification official. Jerusalem was annexed. A new phase of Palestinian nationalism had begun. Guerrilla organisations were formed. Despite that, Jerusalem was changing quickly. The Jewish Quarter in the old city was being rebuilt. New neighbourhoods were being thrown up around the city to make repartition physically impossible. It was safe enough for a school trip to Israel to go ahead. Mr Chapman, the history teacher, was guide-in-chief.

The party of 26 boys spent two days in Tel Aviv, two days in Galilee and a day at Masada. Via the snake path, the boys climbed up to the fortress. As the thermometer stood at fifty degrees, the boys saw the rampart on which the Romans had mounted siege towers for the final assault. The old ruins of Masada resonated with the last-ditch resistance of its defenders and their decision to put each other to death rather than let themselves be taken.

In the culmination at Jerusalem, most of the sites were included in the itinerary. The boys saw the memorial that was a half mountain; Yad Vashem redolent with the most shocking descent into the heart of darkness that history had ever known. And to think it was less than thirty years before. That evening, they discussed the effect it had on them. Mr Chapman described the flapping of bodies of lynched boys on trees in the Deep South of America or the marches of the Civil Rights movement he had witnessed personally five years previously. His black American friends said that if you assert a right to be here, you challenge the entire power and value structure of the Western World. 'The root is rage', the writer James Baldwin had written. Bill sat incredulously as this was related one evening. He could not understand the hatred that white people had for black people and the rage against those who paid for the way of life and prosperity white people enjoyed. Bill had a dim perception that the loss of his own mother fused at some level with the stirring of a social conscience. He would have no problem in having a black lady for a wife one day.

The last day began with a walk along the rampart on top of the Old City Walls. A guide explained how General Gordon of Khartoum suggested Jesus had been crucified on the hill opposite the Damascus Gate. Some of the boys agreed the shape did resemble a skull; Golgotha, in the Aramaic language. Others were not so sure. Under expert tutelage, the boys saw the Western Wall, the last remnant of the Jewish Temple. The Dome of the Rock and the Temple Mount stood as dominant monuments of wounded history over the Jewish Quarter to the west and the Arab Quarter to the north. Through the Old City and then they retraced the pathway of Jesus on the way to crucifixion. It was while walking down the Via Dolorosa that a group of three of the schoolboys muttered mutiny and conspiracy.

"How many more sights are we going to see?" Steve could still hear himself groaning.

"It's doing my head in, all these places of interest," said Jack with his usual melancholy.

"I'm bored," agreed Bill. "I don't want to stay at the hotel for another of those talks put on by old Cruikshank," he said, disgusted. "Fancy doing that to us on our last night! Two thousand years of Jewish history in two hours!"

"I have a plan. This is what we're going to do," said Steve. And so it was agreed.

They would go off in search of adventure that evening. A bar? A nightclub? This was their last night in Israel. Let whatever come that would come. Mr Chapman, the schoolmaster in charge of their group, would no doubt kick up a stink. The conspirators plotted to slip away after the evening meal at the hotel.

The boys wandered through a Jewish Quarter covered with elusive mystery. Through the Arab Quarter and the Damascus Gate they went, in search of a nightclub and adventure that was proving unexpectedly tantalising. But they found themselves in a bar and stayed there for a while. Steve purchased some cigarettes from a market stall. As they sat there, puffing away, they seemed to have found the trap door that emerges into manhood.

It was 9.45 when their adult reverie was shattered. Mr Chapman was looking at them through the window of the bar. There was no escape. He had come for them. "I'll deal with you later!" he said.

The boys knew they were in for it, though they secretly loved Mr Chapman. He was the best of a bad bunch. Having a son a couple of years younger than them helped him get on their wavelength. He frogmarched them along the road and then made a fateful decision. They would return to the hotel by bus.

As these scenes moved by his memory like an old film, poignant with tear-jerking emotion, Steve wanted to run to the front of the cinema screen in his mind and say, "Stop the film. Stop the film!" as if he was hailing down a taxi.

What would anyone do if they knew they had only four minutes to live?

In slow motion, in the film of memory, he sees the face of a terrorist appear at the entrance of the bus and a small object of terror thrown to the back where the boys sat. To his dying day, Steve would remember horror erupting volcanically. There was no escape.

Roll the film on two eternal seconds. Most days, the look on Chapman's face was one the boys saw when they shaved. Bill, Steve and Jack looked again at the face of a fedayeen, who had appeared in the door of the bus, throwing to the back a small dark object of destruction. "Grenade!" shouted a passenger, but the stampede from the front of the bus was not going to allow any escape for passengers at the rear. Horror built up in their voices and on their faces as they remembered the almost involuntary action of their teacher throwing himself on the grenade. 'NO, NO, STOP THE FILM'. It would be there before them once again, the 30 centuries, or was it only 30 seconds, before the explosion, Mr Chapman's face looking at these boys for half a lifetime, willing them to live though he would not. For a long lingering eternity, they looked at each other, the sacrifice and the freed, rescuer and rescued. For one long, lingering moment, the boys watched, transfixed by the volcano horror that had engulfed them from nowhere. Statuesque, rooted by terror, they looked at Mr Chapman and he looked at them, the face of their conscience forever. It took a long lingering moment for the grenade to go off. Absorbing the fatal impact, Mr Chapman's body dissolved into a living flame, the sacrifice wholly consumed on the altar.

Bill looks up at the film. "Will Mr Chapman please reappear? Whose is this thick red sticky blood moving over us?"

Frame by slow frame, Steve sees a bustling street erupting into chaos. He sees dozens of screaming people showered with glass, the air filled with black smoke and sharp with the smell of an explosion; he sees bystanders running and shouting.

Jack had to have glass shards removed from his leg. A passer-by endeavoured to stem the blood with his handkerchief. They all went temporarily deaf with the loudest noise they had ever heard before silence descended. Thankfully, miraculously, the boys suffered minor injuries.

"How that incident shaped my life," Steve thought, as he finally stopped the film.

"The Romans believed that if my name is on someone's lips, I'm still alive. Maybe Chapman is still alive somewhere. I don't think I am," he whispers.

Chapter Twelve:

The Future of the Handshake and a Time of Re-birth

At last, things were easing up.

The survivors began to emerge from their holes and jump into their cars that in many cases had been as redundant as the numerous workers laid off. Though connected with the outside through a daily walk, TV and the increasingly ubiquitous social media, it seemed at times as if the external world of people and things did not exist, that we were stuck in a matrix of our minds like brains in a vat and that all that existed was virtual. But now, blinking at the warm sun that blanketed the landscape of time for day after day, the survivors could glimpse an Aristotle world of sunshine and only banished shadows. There was an external world all right – but was it all right? Gradually, we were allowed to mix but not mingle, to come together but stay apart in the weird paradoxical concoction of those days. Were we ready for the next bit of normality after three months? Spaced queuing, one-way systems and the weary, wise social distancing shaped the return of cultural life. How many lives and how many businesses had not made it through the first half of that strange year of 2020?

Hope was in the air. Most people were all right. But was the economy going to be on life-support? Far fewer were fighting for life's vital breath as the deadly virus started to run out of new people to bite and control. But over in America, a Minneapolis man could not breathe: choked to death by a warrior cop with a foot on his throat and an amoral look on his face at those who made sure the images went viral. This was a pandemic of the spirit.

By now confirmed Zoomers for private as well as work life, Beth and Bill spoke often and then daily. An Atlantic Ocean emotion no longer separated them and neither did the years solidify their different worlds as they once had. Then, one evening, she had some news.

Beth – Hi Bill!

Bill – Beth! Lovely to see you. We haven't spoken since the last time!

Beth – Haha. Not since yesterday. How have you been today? How was the conference?

Bill – Nothing much to report for me. Taking part in a virtual gathering was split-level reality. You are there but not there. You miss the chit-chat of coffee and cocktail commentary. And it shifts the consciousness sideways to see yourself looking at you looking at me.

Beth- Sounds like alternative reality. Sadly, my cleaner has passed away.

Bill – Oh, no. You told me she was dangerously ill with Covid.

Beth – Well, it's finally happened. I feel really gutted.

Bill – So sorry, love. She didn't have an easy life, did she?

Beth – Certainly not. As a black girl growing up in the Civil Rights era, she could never understand why white folk would call the police if her dad went for a walk in the local park or why he had to wait ages for a taxi that would show up within minutes for a white guy. She still had to walk down a street in a white enclave and face the whispers or angry looks. Her brother is incarcerated to this day. He got typecast after being picked up for nothing.

Bill – We hoped this everyday racism would have died by now. At its heart is the superiority of my life is more important than yours because of your skin colouring. You just don't count.

Beth – For people who look like me, it's the privilege of not having to be subjected to it that makes it appear subtle. For her, racism came to her doorstep. Children didn't want to play with her because they thought she looked like faeces. It has been part of the lingo and the dialogue in her family most days. So, hope conditions have been created for creative change.

Bill – This horrible George Floyd episode reveals the deep wound across society that's like pus seeping out. It needs healing, but first off, it needs deep cleaning. It's just brought out what black people have been feeling for years. I tell you, Beth: this is surely a time of re-birth.

Beth – Do hope so. At this moment, there are processions of demonstrators outside the window that have become a regular occurrence. How did it happen that in the midst of the pandemic, that video goes viral?

Bill – Katie says it sums up how black people have long been smothered by systemic racism.

Beth - I still feel strongly about this but not sure I have the fight to make this my fight now.

Bill - Katie does though. Though she never had to experience being told, 'no blacks, no dogs' when going to rent somewhere, Katie struggled to get a job. She says people have very different personal experiences with the law, getting stopped. Her big mantra is that if we're white, it's not what you have to go through but what we don't have to go through that shows up racism in dark colours. She hopes the anti-racism leads to lasting transformation.

Beth – As do all! What does she think about getting rid of statues as symbols of oppression?

Bill – That they stay as object lessons saying 'this is how it started–this is where we are now.'

Beth – A wise young lady! Bill, can I change the subject? I've given in my notice as I told you.

Bill – Big day, Beth! Congratulations for finally taking the step.

Beth – It certainly is. I wasn't getting much work anyway and money is tight.

Bill – Beth, I've been thinking too since you told me you were going to do this. Why don't we join forces at long last? There's something strong and enduring about what we've got that the years and three thousand miles of water could never manage to overcome.

Beth – Very tempting, Bill. Let something good come out of this crazy time just like it did out of the Aids plague and Katie came into our lives. Oh, bless you....

Bill – Yes, my eyes are filling with tears but they are moist with happiness!

Beth – For me as well!

And so plans began to be laid. Katie was thrilled. There were choices to take and moves to make. Bill wondered about telling his old partners in crime. He knew, though, that Liam would be delighted. Liam could be relied on to come forward with empathy.

The taste lingered for two weeks. Liz said she wouldn't move back in straight away. Craig came over as well. But one evening, Liz was late for an arrangement they had made. Jack was cross. This time, it was volcanic. "Do you know how long I've been waiting here?" he exploded. Liz hadn't seen him angry like that since Timothy had burnt a hole in the sofa with his cigarette. Normally, Jack was so placid, far too placid for her. Now, with emotions on both sides rising to the surface, Liz remembered how she had slipped out of love with him. A romantic evening was definitely out for the night.

"Goodbye!" she shouted, slamming the door and leaving Jack stunned by the turn of events.

"Oh, come on, Jude," he protested. But Jude's pride wouldn't let her turn round and Great Alex didn't know how to run after her.

Two weeks went by. Jack bought the computer game that had gone straight to number 1 that autumn in the CD Rom charts. The Sims allowed players to recreate their lives in virtual suburbia. Everyone was doing it. But Jack was hollow. A second- hand life no longer had any attraction for him. Jack's roses were returned. "It's not going to work, Jack," wrote Liz. "Life was easier in our virtual relationship. There are too many emotions in the way. Let's be internet friends again."

Great Alex: Hey Jude. Guess who?

Jude: I can guess. How are the roses?

Great Alex: Fading fast; hope that's not a parable. How was your day, by the way?

Jude: Well, the boss is still a pig.

Great Alex: My new boss just doesn't know how to say sorry when he walks all over you.

Jude: Do you expect him to?

Great Alex: Maybe not. It's on my wish list in my virtual world.

Jude: All the best things only happen in the virtual world.

Great Alex: Like us, for example?

Jude. Is there a place for us in the real world?

Great Alex: To step into the real world is too messy and mature.

Jude: It's much less complicated like this.

Great Alex: But nothing is solved, nothing resolved.

Jude: And all the possibilities are left unopened, like your present.

Great Alex: Liam tells me there's a way into the real world.

Jude: Which way? Down?

Great Alex: He says it's along a road called forgiveness.

Jude: See you around the cyberworld, Jack.

Great Alex: Jude, Jude? Are you there? For God's sake, Liz.

But Jude had disappeared. And the sound was broken by sobbing. It would happen. He knew that. But it would take time.

Liz: Jack. It's me again.

Jack: Well, hello stranger. I've not heard from you for three months.

Liz: I needed time to think whether I'm ready to try again with you.

Jack: I sent you all those messages. They came straight back from the server.

Liz: I changed my email address. It was such a shock finding out it was you. I wasn't sure if I could trust again. I just had to slam the door shut.

Jack: Ok - never asked you. What did you think when you found out it was me all the time?

Liz: I was angry. And I was amused. And I was frustrated- at different times.

Jack: But were you secretly pleased?

Liz: OK. The truth. Take away the shock and yes I was.

Jack: So was I. I suspected for ages.

Liz: I wanted it to be you. But when it really was, I was afraid it couldn't work.

Jack: There's a very odd feel to our relationship, don't you think?

Liz: Maybe it's Millennial madness.

Jack: What does that feel like?

Liz: I couldn't tell you. I wasn't here the last time.

Jack: Instead, tell me what the end of our relationship was like for you.

Liz: When there seemed no prospect of reconciling our differences, I was in a state of shock. One minute I was crying, then I was shouting at everybody.

Jack: For me came the anger. I'd lash out at anything going. Then came the pain.

Liz: I see we're using proper names, not nicknames.

Jack: Maybe we've come out of our virtual world.

Liz: Is there a real world for us, where we can be who we really are?

Jack: The real world is much harder. We have to face up to our disappointments, break free from our utopias and look life in the face.

Liz: Alex told Jude that his relationship broke up because two people couldn't stop hurting one another. Can we forgive each other?

Jack: I think we should meet up.

Liz: Until recently, you wouldn't have wanted to meet me. I had put on so much weight these past few years, I needed to put a zip on my mouth. But just lately, I've lost pounds without hardly trying. I still love you. (I think). How's Steve and Mandy by the way?

Jack: Liz, I have a suggestion; what about coming to our Christmas reunion soon?

In the dying days of the second millennium, Steve was relieved that at least Mandy hadn't reacted against the note he had left on her pillow inviting her to a crisis session tonight. Then Amanda entered the room in her wheelchair, flat and defeated but with a soft entry that made both men wonder if she had been listening outside, so quietly did she enter.

"Hello," she said, with a voice drained of emotion and a face to match, refusing Steve's glance. She eased herself onto the sofa.

"Can we talk?" asked Liam gently, hoping that her troubled soul was preparing for re-entry from prison. But silence. Nothingness. No emotion.

"It's obviously come to a head," said Steve heatedly. "You've been building up to this. Get it out. Let the volcano burst!"

Then tears flowed, gently at first but soon with sobs that shook Amanda. Her body was about to break in half. Steve reached out to hold her but his touch was unwelcome. After a while, Amanda's lips moved. To begin with, Steve was in the third person. He listened impassively. Words came slowly, haltingly at first, but gathered strength as a trickle turned into a tributary.

"I need to start at the beginning," Amanda said, between deep sighs of grief. "I became involved with a professor at Law College. For two years we were together. I was lonely when I wasn't with him."

"His responsiveness to me made me feel noticed, enjoyed and valued. Then he began to look down on me. I was just a silly girl to him."

Steve sat outwardly still, wondering why an old familiar story should rise up and bite him.

"We all want to love and be loved, I guess," said Amanda. "Deep down, that's what I was looking for. On a good day, I was alive. On a good day," she underlined. "It couldn't have worked. He lost interest and moved on. Then I met Steve one night at a disco in Chinatown. He was seeing the sights of San Francisco and already dreaming of his start-up. We got talking. At first, I thought nothing could change the way we felt about each other. Then Steve proposed to me. It was dreamy. We were invincible; we were a team."

Steve nodded. He noticed that a dreamy look had enveloped her like a sheet despite anger.

"Steve was a perpetual adolescent. He had a bruised childhood, the legacy of a domineering mother and a father who was emaciated in the war. You were quite remote when we first met," she said. It was the first time she had spoken to Steve directly for three days. He was counting.

"I think you found my strength both comforting and intimidating. I was the rock. I drew you out. Until then, you had been unable to express your feelings. Before long and hey presto, you were transformed into the most romantic man I've ever known. We were engaged. You were involved, solicitous, considerate."

Amanda suddenly shouted in anger.

"That's why it bloody well hurt so much, don't you see? I was the one that opened the book. You did that for me too. But then you lost interest."

Steve averted his eyes from her. Amanda quietened down.

"On my wedding day, I trembled with the sheer joy of existence. I learnt to cherish each moment. We couldn't have any of our own at first but children loved to be in Steve's company. In spite of being this successful businessman, he was like them in so many ways. Then Jane came along unexpectedly. I went to Steve and said 'I'm pregnant'.

"You can't be. That's not possible," he said, disbelievingly. We had stopped going for any more tests".

Steve enjoyed the memory. His eyes lit up in fond recollection.

"I felt so alive when our children came along," he said. "It seemed natural to renegotiate the relationship, to give up a free-wheeling existence for the sacrifice of having kids. We would be the ultimate parents in training. But somewhere along the line, I think we had a bypass operation from each other."

Amanda nodded as the tears flowed once more.

"Gradually, all your time disappeared in building up your business. We had our differences. You began to withdraw your affection for longer and longer periods. I couldn't stand it when you did that."

Then came a pause in her story; a pause that lasted for three centuries.

"Mind you, I changed too. The woman you married had gone. A mother had replaced her. Like most men, you wanted mothering. You used to complain I put the children first. I should have put you first. Things would have been different now."

"No, no." Steve shook his head strongly, not wanting to be let off the hook.

"But," said Amanda, "don't think I didn't know about those one-night stands. Your excuses were paper-thin. If you're going to tell a lie, at least make it convincing. But you always came back."

"I used to extol the virtue of being true to myself," said Steve dejectedly, with the air of a man waking up to the emptiness of his whole philosophy. "I never pretended to be something I wasn't. The worse crime was to lecture people about morals or religion."

But Amanda didn't seem to have heard his familiar disclaimer of moral unpretentiousness. Now, her words were coming quickly.

"I honestly thought you would never want to detonate your family just for a rough and tumble between the sheets. I told myself again and again that we had a strong enough bond between us to ensure that our marriage was solid."

Amanda looked up, her face wincing with unforgotten rejection.

"Then you met Beth. Why did you have to fall in love with her?"

Steve time-travelled back to their first encounter. Was it his fault he had fallen deeply in love with Beth? He seemed to bump into her. Everywhere, there she was, everywhere he found her. She was so lovely; a living emblem of another world. It went deep. He hadn't planned to fall in love. But what he had with Beth couldn't be denied. He shook himself. Reality drew him back to the present. Amanda went on.

I thought the crash really changed things," said Amanda. But you had to go back to her, didn't you? You just couldn't keep away. And then I found out you got her pregnant!"

Steve looked at Amanda, speaking softly;

"Looking back, that slide down the hillside was a turning point. You were the book I had left behind all those years, barely having started to read. An enormous regret swept over me. I had consigned you to the outermost darkness of being unread."

"When I went back to see Beth," he continued after a pause, "it was to say goodbye. But I got drawn in. I couldn't help myself. She had stopped believing I would leave you but she was determined to have something of me that was permanent. She stole it."

"Stole it?" asked Amanda in disbelief.

"No, I gave freely. But we both knew it was for the last time. I had made my choice to stay with you. But I couldn't help myself."

"We're talking about your child she was carrying," said Amanda, shaking her head, anger combining with tears, hands beating against him. At least Steve wasn't dishing out paper lies.

But who would now be the first to break unending silence?

Steve spoke. "Well, now we've brought all this out into the open, what's the script?" he wondered. "I wish there was some way of putting my life into reverse gear. Why do the invoices seem to come to the wrong address? I never intended Amanda to suffer. I need her to forgive me. Your trust is worth a great deal to me," he said.

A quiet voice spoke up from the depths of the sofa.

"I can put the past behind but it's going to take a lot of time to recover the amused intimacy we once knew. I need somewhere to dump the anger and injustice that shrieks down here. Or the protest I feel will howl like our first Labrador often did when it cried to come back in. You remember the Labrador?"

"Yeah. Jooey? Chewey? Whatever did we call that four-legged monster?"

Liam rose and left them to it. He said goodbye. Steve shook his hand.

"Look, thanks for coming. I think we can take it from here. The odds in favour of us staying together have just improved. We've made a start towards a reconciliation that's real. I guess" he added as an afterthought, "forgiveness couldn't begin until we could acknowledge between us that something had happened. Painful honesty was needed; we couldn't just brush it off like old Joey used to, having a good shake".

"It had to be acknowledged," said Liam simply, "like an invoice that begs to be opened. See you around. Call me if you need me," he said. "Let me know if the restaurant boat is still on."

"Will do," said Steve. "The invoice had to be opened," he repeated to himself, glancing at a couple of brown envelopes that had arrived in the post, bills that wouldn't go away.

They say a sure sign that business is booming in central London is to count the number of cranes. Steve Bright stands in his Canary Wharf office, crane-spotting. Cranes to the left of him, cranes to the right. Was it 38, 39 even? And why had Beth phoned today, leaving a message with his secretary? He looks at his watch. It is time to go to the reunion dinner.

By eight in the evening, the last guests have arrived. Liam is delayed. The tube has unaccountably stopped for ten minutes. Hastening down from Charing Cross to the Embankment, he quickly finds the restaurant boat, shows his invitation to a man with a beard and bow tie and makes his way down a corridor lined with tarpaulin. A young Greek looking lady welcomes him aboard and shows him to the area booked for the occasion.

It was a fine night in December 1999. The lights on the south side of the Thames projected splashes of colour as if on a Monet canvas. Gentle piped music that wasn't out to assault the senses floats through the restaurant and disappears into the guests. Steve Bright, deep in conversation with Bill, glances up and comes to shake his hand.

"Glad you could make it! Welcome. We're all here. I think you know everybody."

Steve ushered him to a seat beside Amanda. On one side of a long table there sat Jack and Liz, and on the other, Bill. They greeted one another.

"Jane is going to be baby-sitting," Amanda was saying about the pre-millennial eve. "She put her name down when she thought she could collect a two-hundred-pound fee. Doesn't seem likely now."

"Are you going to the Dome?" Jack asked.

"No, we couldn't get tickets," Steve replied. "But we'll be there somewhere amongst the three million expected in central London."

Liam looked at them all with great affection, these friends that he had got especially close to in the last three years of his journey, sharing their joys and sorrows; the ebbs and the flows of lives tense with anger, tenderness and guilt. He had read the script, populated by characters struggling to survive experiences, painful with failure.

Jack occasionally glanced at his surprise date, who had been warmly welcomed by Steve and Amanda. The run-down man had found himself and found her in the process. How difficult it had been to learn to trust others, to realise his own competence or to sustain relationships that worked, condemned to second-class mediocrity - or was he? Jack looked convivial enough over the meal table but still occasionally smoked with resentment against a brother who had usurped him. And Liz, haunted by the ghost of failure that wandered the corridor of her mind, riddled with guilt because of Timothy, unable to let herself off the hook.

Amanda said something to Steve but there was clearly lingering tension between them still. Steve was softer now, ever the genial host, laughing, joking his way through life. But to the knowing observer, it was clear that Steve and Amanda were burdened, burdened with the weight of an imperfect relationship and a past that left much unresolved.

And for Bill to be let off the hook for the death of his wife would have been too cheap at any price. It would constitute another betrayal. AIDS had not yet brought Ali's life to a full stop, but Bill was getting support from Beth. She would help him. They'd help each other.

Dinner was served. Pre-dinner drinks were supplemented with the Green Muse. Absinthe, the fin de siècle drink of Paris a century before, was making a comeback. Laughter flowed over the old friends like a Thames tide. They all look so smart, so genuinely pleased to see each other, Liam thought.

"I wonder if they know what secrets each is carrying, and if they know I know?"

For an hour or more it went on. Although enjoyable, knowing something of their inner life, to Liam it was also an evening bathed in pathos. He saw old friends playing out lives with memories, aspirations, unrealised dreams, the fragile happiness, lost opportunities and wrong turnings. Here they were, garrulous about the past, re-living their adventures, re-constructing history. Tension mounted within him. He knew what they could not articulate, of an experience that had affected their lives so deeply that it was calling to them across the years. The shared experience that he knew must come out lay heavy upon him. His stomach began to churn as if he'd eaten something that disagreed with him. His churning grew worse - the knots, the burden, the pain mounted.

And here came the sound of the Beatles drifting unmistakably through the restaurant boat.

"Yesterday, all my troubles seemed so far away. Now it looks as though they're here to stay. O I believe in yesterday."

Jack and Liz looked at each other, eyes smiling and began to sing softly. "Why she had to go I don't know, she wouldn't say. I said something wrong, now I long for yesterday."

"Earlier this year, it was voted the most memorable song of the century. It's been the most widely recorded song in popular music," Jack remarked.

"1965," said Amanda. "So much has happened in our lives."

"It was a good year," agreed Steve. "That's when we started at the school. " And with that, the guests fell silent.

"Just look at us," remarked Bill after a pregnant pause. "Perhaps life would make more sense if we lived it backwards!"

Steve dropped his avuncular, genial host hospitality and grew serious. "There comes a point of muddied realisation that the road will not be so long as we first thought. The journey will be over and all too soon we start asking ourselves what will be our legacy to those that come after. He gives voice to what is in his head – though much remains hidden.

"So many travellers on this strange journey of life exhaust themselves on the senseless pursuit of material possessions and finish without finding spiritual capital."

"It's a spiritual crisis, really," adds Liam. "Live, fling, do the things you always wanted to do while there is still time and youth has not yet fled in embarrassment. But there are other travellers who seek healing from the pain of life and the baffled perplexity that haunts us all, for whom the answer lies in a difficult trip back to the beginning of the journey. Maybe we need to understand the road we've travelled."

Liz was easily swayed by the reflective mood. "It's always hard, I think, to turn round and begin to work against patterns that have moulded us. Difficult but not impossible, otherwise no one could ever dare to be different and get away with it. Just look at us now. So, here we are, children of the permissive age, raised amidst the distinct tremor of social and moral earthquake and the crumbling of values and institutions."

"All that did indeed shape us," agreed Amanda, finding the nostalgic mood hard to resist. "There was plenty to take the shine off. But, in turn, Jane's generation has been shaped by high unemployment, family breakdown, loss of community and environmental nightmares. Not to mention a revolution in communications impossibly futuristic when we were kids. What kind of a new century will it be that Ali's little girl will grow up in?"

"Katie, is it?" she asked Bill. He nodded.

"I would love it that I could adopt her formally but that's another road to travel."

Steve held Mandy's arm and looked at her with affection.

"But, of course, there's something else that has defined our lives," said Jack.

The dinner party went quiet once again. Each man in that restaurant boat was sailing away to a stormy sea of memories, without immediately comprehending they had reached the same destination. Among the three men, or was it four, scenes flashed, a searing experience that bound them together in bonds of blood.

"We have never talked about Israel," Steve observed, breaking cover.

Suddenly, it was there before them like a funeral bell tolling. They remembered the headmaster expressing the grief that the staff and everyone in that school were feeling, grief that had turned to anger. "If it wasn't for you running off like this, it would never have happened!"

And many other words from their compatriots; "It's your fault...you're responsible". Words that had shut them up in a sealed room, unable to talk about it since or resolve the guilt that had hounded them like stubborn dogs for 28 years. Their parents had been unable to face the school again. The boys had been put into other schools. Impact was momentous.

"I believe this group of men is bound together by a shared secret," said Amanda.

"There's definitely something here," said Liz. "Come on, out with it!" she said.

And out it all came, bit by bit, as if each of the men was adding bricks to a Lego house. The evening of exploration despite the warnings not to go off by themselves, sarcastic and caustic comments they all made against the teacher in charge of their group, painted in the unwelcome colours of a jailer.

"He chose to do that for us," said Bill. "He knew if he took the blast, we would be all right."

"How much has that moulded our lives," Jack observed.

It was now Steve who, pointing to Liam said, "We've spoken what has been unspoken between us all these years. I have a hunch that now we've brought it out into the open at last, this is going to be the final reunion, the last supper. Anything you want to say?"

Liam nodded. He had been half-expecting to say a few words. He waited until the waiter cleared the table and served Beaujolais to the assembled guests.

"The individual journey we make," said Liam slowly, "is indeed shaped by the events of the day. But it's also moulded by the choices of every day. These are the real defining moments; what we do with the legacy we are given. But the question I have is whether it's really possible to put right the past? Do we remain bits of inert plasticine, moulded by the choices we made and the events that weathered us? Or can we begin a different journey? What happened outside Jerusalem left an indelible mark on all our lives."

It struck the lawyer in Amanda that he said 'our' lives. Why would he say that?

Liam paused for a minute, as the music played on.

"I'm glad you've asked me here and to say a few words tonight by way of reflection," he concluded. "There's something you need to know about me. As our paths began to cross, and you were beginning to come back into each other's lives again, I knew there was a significance. You see, what took place in Jerusalem has affected us all, me as well as you."

"You? Why you?" five voices exclaimed in near unison.

"Before I was adopted, my name was Chapman. I was the son of your teacher who lost his life in Jerusalem so long ago." As all those years ago, it was a moment to freeze the frame.

"Lost? No," Liam adds. "That's not quite right. He gave himself for you: his life for your life. Every life can be redeemed. That blood upon you all lays claim on you but in a positive way."

One by one, they looked at each other before hugging; their eye contact genuine and warm. Then they gathered round Liam and embraced silently, tearfully. It was the dream-coat Joseph making himself known to his brothers after many years.

For a while after that, they sat in silence, absorbing news on this scale. Bill, Jack and Steve look at Liam and he looked at them; not the face of their accuser but of their forgiver, as of one who sacrificed himself for them and redeemed their lives. It was the teacher back from the dead, come to acquit them. And round the table in that restaurant boat, they linked hands along with Liz and Amanda and Liam prayed softly for them, speaking powerful words.

"Let's go back to my hotel for coffee," said Bill with sudden decisiveness.

And so, they wandered the embankment and found their way back to the hotel. Steve lagged behind, making calls on his mobile phone.

As they asked Liam about his father, his sense of grief from long ago was stirred like an old wound being reopened. He had thought it all resolved and settled. But speaking of the loss churned it all to the surface once more. There was no retreating to a safe world. The ancient wound went deep, as deep as anyone had ever gone. He didn't know they made drill bits that bored so far into the earth.

Then Steve made an announcement.

"My old friends," he said, stirringly, "I feel there is something we need to do. And as I was the one who led us into these waters, will you allow me to help find a way through?"

"What do you have in mind brother?" asked Jack.

"Look, it's Friday evening. I think most of you are staying around this weekend. I am going to propose that we fly to Jerusalem and make our peace with the past in the very place where it all happened."

There are whistles round the room.

"A pilgrimage, you mean?" wondered Bill.

"I suppose so," said Steve. "Why not? We'll know whether the question our friend here has posed can be answered. Can we put right the past?"

"But what about flights?" Jack said. "I'm in, but with the millennium, Jerusalem will be heaving with visitors."

"I would have thought so. But it so happened that a Jewish member of staff went to Israel today to see his ageing mother. We all said the flights would be jammed but the big rush is next week. There are tickets available before the storm. I've checked and they're holding four tickets for all the men here. I'll pay."

"That include me?" exclaims Liam. "What about accommodation?"

"All arranged if you're up for it. It's the Jerusalem Towers Hotel again."

The whole idea seems eerie, stunning. The world was moving too fast. But as they considered it, there was nothing in the way. The women acquiesced, sensing it was important that Jack and Steve abandon their small engagements for the weekend and come to terms with the past. It was something they needed to do. Steve phoned back to confirm. By four in the morning, four men were in the airport lounge at Heathrow waiting for the early morning flight to Tel Aviv.

It was ten days later. The wine flowed and the lights glowed in the Bright household too. Amanda surprised herself at how light she felt when she finally let go of her anger. Someone had just snapped old chains. She was free to go.

Jane came over for dinner on Christmas Eve and ended up staying over two nights. She was running into problems at the BBC and wondering about applying for a new media company that had just started out. Relaxing after one of Amanda's gourmet Christmas dinners, they sat together as a family for the first time in six years. Amanda had been counting. Many things that hadn't been said between them were spoken of. Words that had been thrown around the room like daggers were pulled out of their victim and retracted. Steve said he was desperate for them to forgive him for what he had put them all through.

"No worries. You're all right, Dad," said Jane.

A soft glow from the lights above bathed the room as the clock struck nine. It was a father and daughter moment. Jane was in tears as Steve told her about Jerusalem and the visit the four of them had made there.

"I guess we all fail as human beings," she said. "Goodness knows I'm learning that well enough. I don't connect with what has changed you. You've obviously had a powerful faith experience. But it must be nice to find a place where we can forgive and be forgiven and walk away unburdened. Like driving to a council tip and leaving all the black sacks behind."

"To me, it feels like that moment we had renovating the house, stumbling across an antique beam in the dining room and restoring it to pristine glory," said Amanda, enjoying the scene.

"Any unfinished business," she said to Steve, "or can we get on with our lives now?"

"I've written to Beth," said Steve. "I'll show you the contents later when we are on our own, Mandy. There is one thing I can't get out of my mind though."

"What's that, Dad?" said Jane, as they sat and watched Christmas tree lights flickering. For a moment, Amanda thought he was about to get up and pace the floor but he was only leaning forward.

"I keep thinking about that Bedouin woman whose son was killed in Tunisia."

A wistful expression stole over him as if curtains were half-pulled.

"It's not your fault, Dad!" Jane was firm.

"I know that," said Steve. "I'm not trying to soak up any guilt I can find. It's just that... oh, I don't know."

"What?" said Amanda quizzically.

"It's all very well, isn't it, for foreigners to come in and out of a situation like that, as if we are on a bombing mission. No, of course I wasn't responsible. But I was there."

"I think I see what's troubling Dad," said Jane slowly. "You can't rest easy being a part of what happened."

"I suppose that's it," said Steve. "There must be no loose ends dangling in the air."

Amanda looked at them both fondly. Their relationship was being converted from past tense to a gleaming future.

"Dad," said Jane, "as soon as we can in the New Year, why not go to Tunisia and try to find her? I'll come with you. Let's go for it."

"Sounds good to me," said Steve.

"One other thing," said Steve. "I'm thinking of giving up my addiction to office life. Everyone else will eventually. Why not be a tortoise and carry my office world around with me everywhere I go? These days, you can run the world from a yacht in the south seas," he smiled laconically. "I'll stick with the software design company but run things from here. In fact, I'm wondering about disbanding the Canary Wharf office altogether and making us a truly mobile outfit. I want to run my work more by timeless principles, not time-driven priorities."

"Show me your letter," said Amanda later as she and Steve closed the bedroom door.

"Here," said Steve, fishing a sheet of paper from a book he had purchased in Israel.

Amanda sat on the bed and read in silence, communicating her reaction through tears that made rivulets through her mascara face and watered her cheeks.

———————————————

Dear Beth,

You will be surprised after all this time to get a letter from me. I have loved you and will always be richer for it. I can never deny what we had together. My love for you and your love for me brought us a confusing concoction, a mix that was both sumptuous and maddening, a mix of pain and pleasure. We only wanted to bring laughter to each other's faces, but succeeded in bringing tears to each other's eyes.

Three weeks ago, something happened to me in Jerusalem. You will no doubt have heard about it from Bill. His life was touched too. It feels like I've had a bath. All the muck and grime of the past has been washed and I am enjoying the experience.

So where does that leave you? Beth, I am writing to ask if you will forgive me. We embarked on a ride together. I rode up there with you and we reached out to encounter a hidden secret that was missing from our lives. The cost was that I hurt someone I loved very much. You may think I didn't mean all those things I said to you and the promises I made, but at the time, I really did mean them and let my heart speak louder than my head. You deserve better than an oasis that turned out to be a mirage. I really hope that you and Bill can make a life together that you can be openly proud of, a garden that's the envy of all neighbours.

Your friend, Steve

"You should write some of this down," she said the next day. "It might help someone one day, you never know. I'll help if you want me to."

"Maybe," said Steve reflectively. "But if I ever do that, in respect to you, I'll disguise names."

On the night after Steve and his son returned from Tunisia, Steve brought Amanda the roses that he knew she loved so well. Eyes shining, she drew in their scent and received his love that was now fresh to her. She prepared the bed and delicately, with fine hands, placed on it fragrant petals from her favourite roses.

The next few weeks were heavy with the sound of pages turning. Chapters yet to be written were invested with a new plot. Jack found himself surprised at what was happening inside him. Would there be fresh strength rising up in him to retrieve the towel he had thrown in? A new relationship with

Liz, Steve and Craig? No, there was something more. It was lazily watching the airplane movie out of the corner of his eye that he was now free to dismantle the false story about himself he had so carefully devised. The role he had been handed out could now be given back. Emerging into the real world suddenly tasted better than the old virtual world that had let him down.

And that was how, painfully and with quiet steps of trepidation, Jack and Liz began to re-build things. This time, it would stand the test of time. It was redemption's long reach. When a substantial legacy came her way, Liz determined to invest in housing. The opportunity came in the form of a possibility from a property developer to build a house on the strength of a sizeable investment. Liz and Jack needed no second urging. Brick by brick, they built something to last. Craig, by now leading a drug rehab himself, would often join them. When Jack was offered redundancy from the Merchant Navy company he worked for, the package was generous enough to make it viable for him and Liz to take long trips to India. Increasingly, they got involved with some projects to help the Dalit people build self-respect. For those who lived their lives as wallpaper for the higher value people, it was really worthwhile. Jack and Liz felt their lives had been re-routed.

It happened to Bill as he was jogging on Brighton sea-front in that fraught year of 2020. The country could come out. We did not have to be locked up, locked in, locked down anymore.

The feeling that stirred in him caught Bill unawares. It reminded him of jogging on a warm San Francisco morning twenty years ago when he had received a text message that brought him overwhelming joy. He was allowed to adopt Katie! He was going to be her dad. Never had he known such warming of the heart.

In Golden Gate Park, this antidote to the city centre, there came a moment of realisation like seeing the punch-line of a joke, a light-bulb of an insight in which sudden clarity brought a reaction. And as if the joke was extremely funny, the effect on him couldn't be contained. It was too palpable to dismiss. He felt as if he were suddenly implanted in his own body for the first time, though not as a baby, pinching himself in amazement and laughing like parents exploding with wonder at their newborn child, the latest cosmic creation. When he paused for breath, Bill had an urge to laugh out loud. "Just look at it; look at what we have been given. Eyes, ears, fingers, toes, muscles! I can see, jump, walk, run, laugh, cry!"

Bill felt the mystery of a new life fused together, a foetus dividing, breathtakingly, into wonder. A human child was born, the result of nine months of silent, hidden sculpturing, enacting a programme for the formation of a unique person. Skilfully, mysteriously, the instructions know when to build an arm, leg, heart, brain, skin and bones. The hidden work had taken place in each of the million children who would be born before midnight. In years to come, today would be filled with birthdays. He would make all Katie's birthdays magic.

Laughter and tears erupting from a group of children playing nearby made Bill marvel that human thoughts are flushed with emotions. No computer can fall in love or be joyful like this.

He looked around him. To the east were the museums and the horticultural palaces, tea gardens and bandstands. To the right were paddocks, arboretums and thousands of trees running down to the Pacific. Joggers, cyclists, skateboarders and strollers were enjoying the warm spring day. Babies were in their pushchairs, toddlers were taking their first hesitant steps and children were kicking a ball about. Teenage girls were being feted by adolescent boys; emotions and strange impulses rising for the first time. Without even asking, hormones were reconstructing their bodies, leaving them defiant and confused. In the hazy, lazy day, couples were walking, smiling or being cross, exchanging hard words or shy glances. People in midlife were using the park and so were those who were ageing fast, whose bodies were wearing out. The body is, let it be said, a remarkable feat of design engineering; a wonderfully complex piece of machinery with functioning parts that enable their occupants to grow and to go.

"Ok," thought Bill. "We have bones, glands, muscles and genes. But how come we have a spirit? What is the essence of a human being?" he asked himself. "There's got to be more to us than these amazing bodies of ours. Two-thirds water, a pinch of salt; a brew of iodine, chlorine, sulphur, potassium and chemicals worth a few dollars and then chuck in enough iron to make a couple of rusty nails. Is that a human being? Is that what we're worth?"

He asked as he had a thousand times before, though now with new insight. What are the mysterious origins of a being who can even ask such a question? There must surely be a cosmic plan whereby the universe has produced people and come to consciousness. Does the universe value the end product? And how did we come up with concepts of God, physics, trust or love, or was it all the product of chemical reactions? Should we not pinch ourselves, looking at each other to ask in amazement -- "who are we and how on Earth did we get here? There's a story in this realisation waiting to be told. Sometime, I'll work on it.

He continued to jog around the park. A dad! Bill was going to be a dad. He punched the air. And now here he was and Katie was a fine young lady and thoroughly in love. She had come through all the rubbish life had thrown at her and indeed, had turned it all to good effect. When she had become more and more active in social causes during lockdown, especially black lives, she said it felt like receiving the title deed to her house. Though white, in Robert, she had found someone who shared her social passion. They would make a great couple!

It was clear from the outset that there was something wrong. The pre-arranged Zoom rendezvous lacked someone. Bill was wondering if he should share that he and Beth were going to get together. But heck. All that was twenty years ago.

Sensitivity about Steve and Beth should surely have cleared by now. He waited for the old friends to come on. Then two people were in the waiting room seeking admission.

Bill – Jack! Liam! Good to see you. How's everything been in the last month?

Jack – Better now, but Liz and I have had a bad time. Oh, hi, Liam!

Liam – Just caught the end of that. Good evening, everyone. What's been going on?

Jack - Both Liz and I have had more than a brush with coronavirus. It's not been the normal pattern but I think I got off lightly. Liz's coughing fits, though, left her breathless.

Bill – Sorry to hear that, Jack. This is a disease we had never heard of at the start of 2020. Talk about that book, 'The Year of Living Dangerously'.

Liam – Big stress for so many. Bill, I can't help wondering about Beth in New York when I hear the news from America, though. Surge in new cases as we speak.

Bill – Her cleaner died of it last week. Beth feels passionate about the way racial division has always been America's original sin and default setting. She's decided to come over here and join me.

Liam – Wow! That's great Bill. So, so pleased. Why didn't you do this years ago, though?

Bill – I really don't have an answer for you on that. To be honest, and within these four Zoom walls, it was all a fresh defence against the possibility of surrendering again, watching for anyone who came just that bit too close. To abandon her defences was too high a price.

Liam – And now? Beth has always struck me as a locked-up person living a locked-up life.

Bill - I think it's realising she no longer wants to live her life with all those ramparts! What is she doing, she wonders? How long does she want to live life behind careful fortifications?

Liam – I am delighted! If you marry, would love to have the privilege of taking the service.

Bill – That may well happen! Don't know how many guests we are allowed?

Liam – Up to 30 at the moment, but things could change, depending on when it is.

Jack – Never met the lady but I've heard bits about her from Steve. I do, of course, realise that the story he wrote, contributing to our Canterbury Tales, was a thinly veiled autobiography.

Bill – Mine was too and I didn't really reveal my innermost thoughts.

Liam – Finish it sometime, Bill! Maybe before Beth comes over as your time may well be spoken for. By the way, while waiting for Steve, I've been urging people to keep a gratitude journal to record all the positive things each day. Folk write in to our church and say how important it is as well as the online services and things we're doing to help people pray.

Bill – Katie says the future will be kinder than the past. The most treasured things in this world are exchanged, she reckons. They cannot be bought or sold. That's a cause for prayer. She's rapidly acquiring the tools of an activist, by the way, so watch out everybody.

Jack – And while we're about it, pray for India. In Europe, the situation is easing up but over here, the chief minister of Delhi has said the speed at which coronavirus has spread has severely challenged its health system. That's the worst-hit area but where we are, reaching out to Dalit peoples, things are pretty bad. We have been able to distribute food to migrant workers in slums, the extreme poor in rural areas, and most recently, to HIV-affected families.

Liam – Love to come over as soon as we're through all this period of distress.

Jack – Sure. Oh, no!

Liam and Bill – What is it?

Jack – Oh, dear. I've just had a text from Mandy. She says Steve is having heart attacks.

It was true. Steve paused to look up from his office at home, glancing at Amanda pottering around in the garden on a June day as she tended her Queen Elizabeth roses, which had been fading but were beginning to bloom again. The thumping inside his chest grew louder and it felt like his heart was straining to break free. The doctor had been warning him about his angina. No. Not now. Not yet. Please, Lord. More time. More time. Please, Lord.

He tried calling to Amanda, still tending her roses, but no words would form on his lips. He reached out a hand to beckon to her but she didn't see. The pounding continued, a noise as when two railway carriages are decoupled. But even as mind and body had threatened to separate and had come back together, a peace came over him with an exultant sense of homecoming that he could swim in.

And in that moment, time stood still and he understood. He understood that all he had ever worshipped was misplaced yearning. He understood that in all his friendships, he had pined for friendship with the One who made him.

He understood that in every sunrise pregnant with the new day, in every mountain rising into the morning, in every meadow and in every leaf of every tree, he had glimpsed the source of beauty who had endowed the world so generously.

He understood that in every stumbling act of compassion, of forgiveness and mercy he had unwittingly declared that compassion, forgiveness and mercy lay at the heart of all things and were to be prized above gold and silver. He knew now he could exchange a world where roses bloom only for a time for a garden of fresh flowers.

Postscript

One autumn day, Beth walked up the aisle of the church where Liam was minister. Bill was waiting for her. He had waited for many long years and here she was walking towards him, her eyes shining with love. Katie gave her away, but in truth, was maid of honour. The service that Liam took was replete with the most profound happiness. Robert was there but so were Jack and Liz, pleased to come and share the long-awaited joy. Jack read from First Corinthians Thirteen; the most sublime elegy of love ever penned, said Liam as he preached on the love of Christ that redeemed and the blood shed one far-off Friday in Jerusalem. They all watched as Beth and Bill vowed to laugh and weep in the measure that life would take them, until they would come at last with fullness of years and hearts' content to the banquet where the children of God feast together at the Father's table.

There, in the glow of forgiveness, a man and a woman expressed their love in a fire, sometimes soft, sometimes fierce. Whether tired and worn, new or renewed, no one can take this fire to themselves without being singed in its incandescent flame. They melt into one another; snatched moments of eternity that transcend their ordinary existence and propel them forward. The mystery of human loving haunted and taunted them, bound sometimes for glory, sometimes for shame.

Exquisite touch, routine motion, rough handling, the sweet smile of tenderness, boots worn between the sheets; a skill to be learnt; a reunion to be enjoyed. Such is the delicate tapestry woven by the man and the woman as endowed movements of a strange dance become not `mine' and `yours' but 'ours'.

What means this mystery, they think, that a strange force seizes us and extends our bodies in surrender? What complexity of fraught and blessed emotions, awkward tangle of bodies and communication, exchange of vulnerability that strips us and mocks our pretensions? What strange democracy of bonding, this aristocracy of pleasure offered to our common humanity, joining and merging that are a part of the entrancing magic of permanent love?

We walk with a limp that is a constant reminder of our frailty. And we hear from within our own soul the discordant cry that is an echo of heaven or an echo of hell.

Love was made to flower in its proper seedbed. But how is that some have remained a sealed garden, never finding the secret of what opens and closes the door?

"I have come into my garden, my sister, my bride. I have gathered my myrrh with my spices. I have eaten my honeycomb and my honey; I have drunk my wine and my milk."

And in the time of love, a song is born between the man and the woman, a song to be redeemed and treasured and shared without knowing it with lovers across the continents and across the years.

"If I could take a raptured moment and imprison it within a scented memory, if I could hold fast a wave that stirs unannounced from an ecstatic sea, it would be clad in gift-wrapped betrothal and presented to you."

The End

Appendix – poems

(The Beth cycle)

Uncommon Grace (when Bill is blown away with how Beth handles meltdown)

The ordinary waits
It quietly begs to be formed
re-formed
transformed
She gives shape, arranges, re-arranges
Not as a series
Of disconnected acts,
But taking the ordinary
The common field; the grace
Open to all, debarred from none
And invests with uncommon grace
Herself
That which waits to be formed,
re-formed
transformed
Into a field where flowers bestrew her way
Into a field where the diamond is considered ordinary.

Tiny, tiny girl (when Bill first catches eye on Katie)

She held her;
Tired, weary eyes transfixed by gaze
Upon a tiny, tiny girl,
Who emerged from her darkness
Only moments before.
The urge to merge
Blending consummate delight
(Seeing what conjoined selves would do)
With openness to creative possibility
Had led here to tiny, tiny girl,
One and one equals three!
And now we pinched ourselves
With amazement, laughing
Exploding with wonder
At the latest cosmic creation.
Eyes, ears, fingers, toes
The mystery of us fused together
Hidden sculpturing enacting
A programme for the formation
Of tiny, tiny girl!
You held her,
I held her.
'You will be our daughter!'
As in enduring covenant
To tiny, tiny girl!

Weaving her own brand of magic (when Bill returns with Katie to the UK to live and work)

> *Warp and weft*
> *Right and left*
> *Into the room the weaver comes.*
>
> *The room is dark; it stands bereft,*
> *Waiting for the warp; waiting for the weft.*
> *Waiting for the weaver*
> *In anticipation*
> *Who with movement deft*
> *Brings illumination*
> *She who lights up a room,*
> *Any room.*
> *By her arrival.*
> *When she comes.*
>
> *Warp and weft,*
> *Right and left*
> *Interleaving rush and bale*
> *As into its own born form*
> *A pattern emerges,*
> *When she comes.*
> *Into rooms that are sad,*
> *Rooms that are glad,*
> *Rooms that are tragic,*
> *Weaving her own particular brand*
> *Of magic.*

The love of geometry (when Bill thinks of Beth during long years of separation)

> *Not now Euclid, squares and lines,*
> *But non-Euclidean geometry.*
> *The curvature of space and time*
> *That marks her joyful symmetry.*
>
> *The soft dream that travels*
> *From mound through navel*
> *To mountain peaks sublime*
> *Then below to hidden cave*
> *The curvature of space and time*
> *Her mysterious allure, her beauty*
> *By sensibility defined.*
>
> *Dream-tracing ahead of the curve,*
> *Measuring the tingling of the nerve!*
>
> *Her look, the anvil of desire*
> *The passion that will burn like fire.*

The hundred days (a hundred days after Bill realises he loves Beth deeply)

When you entered the room,
Conversation fell silent
And buses paused outside.
This speaker too was numb,
As he knew by heightened instinct,
And with sweeping unhesitation
Announcing potency of the heart.

Since then, time has fused chemistry
With mystery.
The strange compelling power
Of a force, deep and profound
That must surely emanate
From deep below ground,
Like a trickle that can grow
Into a river's certain flow.

When we fall in love,
It is as if we see
Someone in their true colours.
We catch sneaking glimpse
Of what they can be
As well as what they are.
So it was with the bright shining
Of you that leads to heart pining
Deep care and regard merging with longing
For the lady magic of you
That has only grown

> *Through deep river channels.*

A day without you is a day ill-spent (when Beth did not come for Easter)

> *A day without you is time ill-spent*
> *I could not give you up for Lent*
> *Without heartache*
> *Or jagged, sandpapered*
> *Feelings to vent*
> *Like a man on a pyre,*
> *Like a bird that sings a solitary song*
> *Waiting with abated breath*
> *For her smile one Advent.*
>
> *The hope no weariness can wain*
> *Or disappointment dent*
> *To take from her company*
> *Love coal*
> *To set her body on fire*
> *And ignite her soul.*

On her humanity

She dwells amidst allure
The imagination glides gently down
Into her softness,
The Christ Spirit of her.
Magnetic strength, compelling
In its unspoken utterance
That can undermine castle walls
Like the most potent of explosives.

But long after we have gone
Separate paths into time's midst
When I see people treat each other
Like e-commerce items they can customise
With a swipe
If I should be tempted
To forget someone's humanity
Or to fool myself into shying away
From a real connection
I will remember her eyes
Patiently locked with mine
Awaiting my response.

This too is temptation
That can undermine castle walls
Like the most potent of explosives.

On being tantalising (the Christmas before, in New York)

Across the table she sat,
As Christmas and birthday
Imperceptibly merged
And the sun was set to stay.
The guests enjoying the urge
For conversational wine.

And as we dined,
She ate and drank
Eyes glistening amidst
A beautifully formed body
And from her busy lips
Came words as sparkling diamonds.

I ate too,
Imbibing the food of love
The loveliness of her.
Longing to make her lips
Busier still,
Out of reach,
But never out of mind,
Tantalisingly near
Tantalisingly far.

The haunting
With unintended allure she came,
A soft glow that touched
The volcanic core of me
Not as a ghost without form

But a real lady beautifully clad
In a real body; fitting clothing
For an inward glow of soul and spirit.
With hair that will dance.
Through future corridors
Lined with memory and imagination.

The country to which we move inexorably
Calls to us, beckons us, haunts us
Sending its emblematic emissaries
Who take many forms, many guises,
To stir with challenging delight
The molten mix of our lives.

The air she breathed was alive
I celebrated rich beauty of mind and form
As through her unconscious ways,
She found the secret of what opened
And star dust (with liberal helping)
Was sprinkled in my eyes
Through her eyes; caverns of mystery.
Her smile, her intelligent warmth
Her humanity, haunting me
Kissing me where soft lips
Never will.
The sky-lighter (when Bill realises Beth will come and join him)
How shall I sing the song
Of the sky-lighter
Whose warm glow of spirit

Lights up the full orb
Of the tender day?

Into my world
The sky-lighter comes again.
Fragrant flowers open their soul,
The birds emerge once more
To sing chirpy love lore
That serenade her.

Send away the clouds
Dismiss the tired shrouds
That throw pale light
Over the world where I live and fight.
The lighting up of sky
Replacing mock solitude of night.
Beauty of spirit
Dreamy body clothing
Stirring, stirring, moving.

Grace of life; prayerful heart
Adorning her.
Lend fresh colour to images
Painted forever on the walls of memory
Of one who lights up the skies of God.
The time-traveller (after a meal out together)
How odd the capacity to jump through time
To leap across months and days
As if there were no barriers, no line
In the sand of the years.

A week. A tiny, unnatural thing
Of significance there is none
Not fixed by the stars
Nor setting of the sun.

Then it was that we drank and dined
'Small bubbles? – or more wine'?
The meal, the starter, the pork,
No longer present but past
Victim of fork

I ate too,
Imbibing the food of love
The loveliness of her.
Longing to make her lips
Busier still,
Out of reach,
But never out of mind,
Tantalisingly near
Tantalisingly far.
I will remember her eyes
Locked with mine
As I spoke
Words of love
Into them
The unmooring
When colours of summer merge into autumn red,
When a black cygnet matures and a swan is born.
When the wind from the north begins to blow
(Stirring restless sea)

Change can be felt in the very air.
Everything is in flux, moving, dynamic,
As space between stars and people who are stars,
No vacuum does it possess.
Pregnant with life, it teems with possibility.

So from her, I feel the electricity
Of a soul radiant with living colour
Unmooring me,
Setting me on a wave crested sea
An intermediary between places, people and all time.

Touched by delight (the morning after their wedding)
Has anyone seen milady?
By day I looked for her
Across landscapes of mind and soul,
Of our labyrinthine labours.
But milady was not there,
Alive with her vivid vivacity
As on that memorable day
Yet absent in a present sort of way.

But in the shades of the night
She was there
Her red dress doffed,
No red breast; tho singing
The robin song of her soul
In a slow movement.
We sat facing
My desire parcelled

To her.
Without front, without clothing
Beautiful curves
Lush femininity
Calling to me, beckoning me
Though I touched her not
Until the time
When with tantric throb
Plateau and peak merged

No nook, no tunnel
Unexplored
Rich lands of soul and spirit
A new chapter of tender passion
In the book of mystery
Rising to urgency and tempestuous passion
In a heaving sea.
Merging with her
With whom I am at my best.
We laugh, we pray
And we are at rest.

9 781913 704339